David grinned. "If that's an offer, I'll take it."

Beneath the knit of his sweater, the muscles of his broad shoulders were knotted and tense. The relaxation came gradually.

"You have . . . wonderful hands."

"You're the one with wonderful hands," Mallory responded. "I noticed them in the supermarket."

"What did you notice?"

Mallory hesitated for a moment before answering. What she'd noticed had been clues to his character as well as physical power and beauty. "I saw your hands looked strong and capable," she said slowly. "Strong . . . but gentle."

He reached forward and touched her face. "The first thing I noticed about you was your perfume," he said. "It was like the scent of springtime as you walked by: warmth, wildflowers . . . woman." His hand slipped around to cup the back of her head. "All woman. Mine . . ."

Other Second Chance at Love books by
Carole Buck

ENCORE #219
INTRUDER'S KISS #246
AT LONG LAST LOVE #261
LOVE PLAY #269

Carole Buck *is a TV network movie reviewer and news writer who describes herself as a "hopeful romantic." She is single and currently lives in Atlanta. Her interests include the ballet, Alfred Hitchcock movies, and cooking. She has traveled a great deal in the United States, loves the city of London, refuses to learn to drive, and collects frogs.*

Dear Reader:

Summer may be ending, but this month's SECOND CHANCE AT LOVE romances will keep the fun alive. We begin with...

Anything Goes (#286) by Diana Morgan. This is the fifteenth romance—but a first for SECOND CHANCE AT LOVE—by this husband-and-wife writing team. And what a zany romp it is! Angie Carpenter, who's just been named Supermom by a national magazine, becomes so incensed by wily inventor Kyle Bennett that she vows to uphold housewives and the American way by beating Kyle's six-armed robot in a televised contest. But she doesn't reckon on falling in love with Kyle! *Anything Goes* boasts what must be one of the most original reasons for interrupting a love scene—Benny the robot arrives unexpectedly to serve lunch! Angie's mortified. You, on the other hand, may never stop laughing.

Poisoned peanut butter may sound like a "sticky" basis for a romance, but in *Sophisticated Lady* (#287) Elissa Curry adds a mouth-watering hero and a never-stuck-up heroine to create a delicious love story. The problem is that Mick Piper's being accused of poisoning his *own* peanut butter (he manufactures the stuff), and Abigail Vanderbine, who's come to interview him and ends up staying, is determined to find out who's really responsible. You'll find Elissa's magic touch in the gleefully witty repartee and oh, so sexy situations. And be sure not to miss the cameo appearance by Grace and Luke Lazurnovich from Elissa's *Lady Be Good* (#247)!

In *The Phoenix Heart* (#288) by Betsy Osborne, proper Bostonian Alyssa Courtney is sure she'll never adjust to laid-back, freaked-out California—especially once she meets gulpingly handsome cartoonist Rade Stone. Suddenly she's living in a state of constant crisis, and falling in love with a man whom her job requires she expose as an evil influence on children! Even her kids turn traitors by being on their worst behavior around Rade. Don't miss this tenderly warm romance filled with laughter and loving.

In *Fallen Angel* (#289), Carole Buck creates a powerfully emotional love story. Beautiful, vulnerable Mallory Victor is caught between two worlds: the upper-crust New England world of hero Dr. David Hitchcock, and the glittery but ultimately shallow world of rock music—where, unknown to David, she induces hysteria in teen-aged fans as rock's "bad girl," Molly V. Using both Mallory's and David's points of view to very skillful effect, Carole deeply involves us in these two characters' dilemma. Carole says *she* cried as she wrote the last thirty pages. Maybe you'd better keep some tissues handy, just in case...

Hilary Cole adds a fresh voice to romances in *The Sweetheart Trust* (#290). Here, the desirous thoughts of two mystery writers put zing into their literary collaboration. Kate Fairchild has already fallen hard for impossibly charming, delightfully unpredictable, infuriatingly witty Nick Trent. When she inherits a decrepit Victorian mansion, she seizes the opportunity to domesticate Nick in a country setting. But rural life includes unexpected—often hilarious—complications ... and none of the guarantees Kate's looking for. Lots of you raved about Hilary Cole's TO HAVE AND TO HOLD romance, *My Darling Detective* (#34). You'll be even more enchanted by *The Sweetheart Trust*.

Finally, in *Dear Heart* (#291) we bring you a delightful new tale from an old favorite, Lee Williams. Why does Charly Lynn gravitate toward children and lovingly nurture the animals in the pet store she helps run? Bret Roberts doesn't have time to find out. He's too busy stealing kisses ... and trying to survive the antics of a hysterical monkey in little red pants who decides to take someone's car for a joy ride on a San Francisco hill! The fact that Bret is allergic to animals—and Charly houses innumerable dogs, cats, a rabbit, and a parakeet in her small apartment—complicates the rocky romance between this hapless couple, who are otherwise perfect for each other. Or almost ... When things get really rough, Charly writes to "Dear Mr. Heart," the local advice columnist, begging for help ... never realizing what further trouble she's getting into!

Enjoy! Warm wishes,

Ellen Edwards

Ellen Edwards, Senior Editor
SECOND CHANCE AT LOVE
The Berkley Publishing Group
200 Madison Avenue
New York, NY 10016

Second Chance at Love

FALLEN ANGEL

CAROLE BUCK

A
SECOND CHANCE AT LOVE
BOOK

To Mom and Dad,
who always believed

FALLEN ANGEL

- 1 -

HE WAS, MALLORY VICTOR decided after careful consideration, the most attractive man she'd ever seen—especially in the frozen foods section of a supermarket. Vacillating between a package of frozen peas with sliced mushrooms and a package of frozen peas with pearl onions, she studied him covertly from beneath long, lowered lashes.

She decided he was probably in his mid-thirties—about six or seven years older than her own twenty-nine. He was a shade over six feet tall, and despite the camouflage of his tan trenchcoat, there was something about the easy, confident way he moved that told her he was a man who kept himself in good shape.

He had thick, sandy-brown hair that was windblown from the inclement, wintry weather. There was a trace of a cowlick on the crown that gave his appearance a hint of ruffled boyishness. He wore horn-rimmed glasses that had slipped down his aquiline nose several times since she'd begun watching him. He always shoved them back into place with an unthinking poke of his right index finger.

He wasn't conventionally handsome. His features were craggy and a bit uneven. One of his eyebrows was a little higher than the other, lending him an enduring look of faintly quizzical amusement. His skin had a healthy, outdoorsy tone, and there was a scar on the stubborn jut of his cleft chin. His expression held a curious mixture of intensity and absentmindedness.

No, he wasn't handsome—not in the way some of the men Mallory knew were handsome. Yet he projected an aura of compassionate intelligence—of utterly masculine gentleness—that Mallory found deeply appealing.

He seemed so assured. So comfortable with himself. So . . . normal.

Mallory dropped two cans of frozen orange juice into her shopping cart, a frown shadowing her gamine features. *Normal*. What did she know about normal after the life she'd led for the past ten years? Normal to her was the rock-and-roll roller coaster. It was an endless blur of one-night gigs, screaming fans, prying reporters, and a multiplying horde of hangers-on. Normal to her was having what should be personal, private moments turned into public circuses.

Normal! What was remotely normal about a woman who hadn't been in a supermarket for four—no, nearly five—years because her last trip to one had caused a near-riot?

Mallory sighed and picked up a carton of frozen pizza. It wasn't on her shopping list, but there was something oddly reassuring . . . something normal . . . about frozen pizza.

* * *

Dr. David Lenox Hitchcock first noticed her in the bakery section, which was one aisle before the frozen foods department. It was her scent—a faint but haunting mix of floral and musk—that captured his attention initially, piercing his normal end-of-a-long-day preoccupation with insinuating delicacy. He caught the subtle fragrance as he maneuvered his cart by hers, his eyes skimming down his scrawled grocery list as he moved. Looking up in response to the perfume, he experienced an instant, inexplicable surge of attraction when he saw Mallory.

She was about five feet five and slender to the point of fragility, although there was no mistaking the femininity of her slim figure. Her clothes—tight jeans, exotic high-heeled boots, and a lemon yellow down jacket—were youthfully trendy, but there was an air of experience about her that said she'd left her girlhood behind a long time before. Her hair was mink brown and fell in a cloud-soft tumble of curls that emphasized her high cheekbones and her unexpectedly provocative mouth. Her eyes—dark, like her hair, he thought—were wide-set and skillfully made up.

But the thing that struck him most forcefully was the contradiction he sensed in her, even at a distance. There was something extraordinarily sensual about her, yet he felt a strange, balancing innocence as well. She radiated poise, yet there was a faintly furtive—almost fearful—air about her, too.

He had a sudden, powerful urge to take that fear away. He wanted to protect her. To release the tensions so plainly locked up within her. He wanted to . . .

You want to what, Hitchcock? he asked himself with an edge of self-mockery. You want to slay whatever dragons the lady has with your trusty stethoscope, then sweep her off in your faithful VW? Where would you sweep her to? Your place is a mess, now that Mrs. Winslow's out with the flu. Plus, the way things have been going lately, your service would phone in the middle of the big seduction scene . . . just as it did last week.

David's mouth quirked into a rueful smile. The lady involved in that particular seduction scene had not been pleased with the interruption—or with his immediate response to the summons it brought. She'd been gone by the time he'd returned from the emergency housecall. He'd accepted her unceremonious exit philosophically. While David Hitchcock was far from a monk—after all, an unmarried doctor with money and a prominent name was the target of a lot of interesting offers and he was only human—he was a doctor first and foremost.

David glanced at the dark-haired woman again. Something told him she might not take kindly to interruptions, either. Something told him she was used to receiving a man's undivided attention.

Who is he? Mallory wondered, picking over the cellophane-wrapped chicken pieces on display in the meat and poultry section of the store.

He was several yards away, looking at ground beef with an air of rapt concentration. He selected one package, put it into his cart, and then wheeled down toward the fish section. The middle-aged butcher working behind the counter gave him a friendly nod of acknowledgment. The sandy-haired man smiled in return. The change of expression was quick but wonderfully warm.

Suddenly Mallory wanted him to smile at *her*. And she wanted to smile back. She hadn't felt like smiling at a man in a long, long time . . .

Oh, look, he has to be married, she told herself. Even if he isn't wearing a wedding ring, he has to be married. A man like him doesn't run around unattached! He's probably buying that ground beef so his wife can make meatloaf for him and their two adorable children.

He had beautiful hands: strong and lean-fingered. She'd

noticed them when she'd checked for a wedding ring. His hands spoke of great power...and infinite tenderness. There was a touch of the artist in those hands, and an impression of controlled, tempered capability as well.

Mallory felt an unexpected and disturbing shiver of excitement run through her. It had been nearly a year since she'd known a man's touch—a lover's caress. Yes, she'd had the comforting closeness of friends and the enthusiastic embrace of an audience, but there had been no one since the death of her husband, Bobby Donovan.

There'd been no one except Bobby when he was alive, either; although, Lord knew, she'd had the opportunity. And, some might say, the justification, given her late husband's infidelities.

"Excuse me?"

Mallory started, her pale face going even paler.

"Yes?" Her voice was low and not quite steady.

The inquiry—two, nonthreatening words—had come from the man behind the counter. He was gazing at her questioningly.

Oh, don't let him recognize me, Mallory prayed silently. There had been a time when she'd dreamed about public recognition. And there'd been a time, once she'd made the dream come true, that she'd delighted in her celebrity. But now...

"You seem to be havin' a hard time makin' up your mind, Miss," the man observed. "Somethin' I can help you with?"

Mallory relaxed a little. He didn't know who she was! He was treating her just like any other customer.

Anonymous. She felt blissfully, blessedly anonymous.

"Miss?"

"Oh—thank you," she said, summoning up a smile. Mallory knew how to use her smile. She could flash it with dazzling brilliance or heat it with sultry invitation. Pulling herself together, she arranged her face into what she hoped was a pleasant, ordinary smile.

"Is there somethin' I can get for you?" the man persisted.

"No, that's all right. I'm just . . . I'm not exactly used to grocery shopping."

That was an understatement. About the only thing she was used to these days was ordering from room service.

"I see." The man nodded. "Well, if you do need anything—"

"Actually—" Mallory darted a quick glance down toward the sandy-haired stranger. She debated with herself for a moment, then gave into curiosity and impulse. "Could you—do you know who that man is? He—ah—looks familiar."

It sounded lame. But, to her surprise, the meat counter man nodded emphatically. "Sure thing. That's Dr. Hitchcock. He's got a practice here in Farmington. My brother's family goes to him."

"Oh. Well—"

"He organized some kind of free medical clinic in Hartford, too," the man went on. "You know—gettin' around all the red tape and bringin' medical help to people who really need it. He got some sort of White House award for that. His picture was in the paper for it. That's probably why he looks familiar."

"That must be it," Mallory agreed. She was impressed by Dr. Hitchcock's résumé—and a little intimidated. "Well, thank you very much." Smiling her appreciation, she picked up a package of chicken breasts.

"Hey, I know what it's like tryin' to place a face," the man answered. "Besides, it's my pleasure to help a very pretty lady."

Lord, she has an exquisite smile, David thought, a rush of liquid heat flowing through the lower part of his body as he witnessed the exchange between the unknown woman and the counterman. And her voice! Thanks to the Muzak piped into the store through the P.A. system, he couldn't make out what she was saying, but he could detect a husky, musical quality in the way she spoke. He could almost imagine the way her voice would sound whispering his name...

Hitchcock, another voice—this one inside his head— whispered, you are cracking up. You're standing in the middle of your hometown supermarket, fondling a piece of semifrozen flounder and fantasizing about a total stranger!

I should introduce myself, he thought wryly. That way I could fantasize about someone I've at least met.

Hell, if I met her, maybe I could do more than fantasize!

Maybe I can ask him to reach something from the back of one of the top shelves for me, Mallory mused. She'd spent the better part of the last ten minutes contemplating, then discarding, a wild variety of schemes for meeting Dr. Hitchcock.

Maybe I can take the crucial middle can out of one of those carefully stacked floor displays and send everything spilling across his path.

No, Mallory, the voice of reason counseled sensibly. Absolutely not.

I can ask her advice about laundry detergents, David reflected.

Or maybe I can impress her with a witty but incisive commentary on the health benefits of polyunsaturated fats.

Suave, Hitchcock, he ridiculed himself without rancor as he pushed his cart down the aisle stocked with soft drinks, beer, and snack foods. That would really be suave.

His jaw jutting with determination, David pulled a six-pack of cola off the shelf. He wedged it into the cart next to the three rolls of superabsorbent paper towels he had no memory of picking up.

What if she were married?

The produce department. They were less than a yard apart. Mallory could feel his eyes on her. She held her breath, a giddy nervousness fizzing through her.

"Excuse me," David said. "Do you know anything about picking pineapples?"

Mallory looked at him. His voice was as warm as his smile. It was beautifully modulated and threaded with humor. She doubted if he'd ever said "babe" or "y'know, man" in his life.

"Picking pineapples?" she repeated. He had terrific eyes. They were a changeable blue-gray. They were perceptive, intelligent eyes. His gaze was very steady as it rested on her face.

David nodded. Picking pineapples was hardly a sophisticated subject for conversation, but at least it had broken the ice. He took a deep breath. The tantalizing scent of her perfume made him feel a little lightheaded.

"What I mean is: Do you know anything about picking out a good pineapple?" He smiled encouragingly. He felt his pulse pick up when she smiled back. There was a tiny, strangely endearing chip in the edge of one of her top front teeth.

"I'm afraid I don't," Mallory admitted reluctantly, hoping her negative answer wouldn't put an end to his smile. It had the same appealing asymmetry as the rest of his features. The left corner quirked up crookedly, bracketed by a deep crease. "I–I do know how to pick out a good cantaloupe," she volunteered. Improvise, she instructed herself, you're good at that.

"Cantaloupes, hmm?" David echoed. "I was wondering about them, too."

Actually he didn't give a damn about cantaloupes. What he *was* wondering about was whether her skin was as petal soft as it looked. He was wondering if her ripe mouth would taste as warm and as sweet as her smile.

"Well, they're not in season right now, of course," Mallory said, filling the brief silence. "But the way you can pick out a ripe one is by pressing the green circle on the stem end. If it gives, the melon's ready. You can sniff that end, too. If you smell cantaloupe, that's a good sign."

"I never knew that." She could have been telling him that cantaloupes were part of a UFO plot to take over the world for all he was registering.

"My husband taught me about cantaloupes," she told him.

That registered. David felt as though he'd been kicked in the stomach.

"Your—husband?"

Mallory recognized his change of mood and stiffened, her expression becoming guarded. "My husband, Bobby," she explained briefly. "He's . . . dead."

For one awful moment, David was afraid he was going to say something like "I'm glad to hear that." Luckily, he was able to control his tongue before that kind of unforgivable—if unpleasantly honest—sentiment slipped out.

"I'm sorry," he said. "Has it been—"

"Eight months. He died in a boating accident." It came out in a rush. She wanted to stave off further questions . . . and answers.

"I see." David acknowledged the information sympathetically.

Mallory cleared her throat. "Does your . . . wife . . . do something special with pineapples?" she asked, inclining her dark head toward the fruit display.

David's glasses started to slip out of place once again. He shoved them back up. "I'm not married."

"Oh." She wondered if there was some kind of polite, proper response to make. She was certain that, 'that's great,' wasn't it. She settled for the carefully neutral *oh*.

"By the way, my name is David Hitchcock." He put out his hand.

Mallory took it. The firm touch of his palm against hers had an electrifying effect on her. It triggered a quiver of sexual awareness that reached clear down to her toes.

The contact affected David, too. Her hand felt cool and fragile in his and he was aware of the stirring of his body as her slender fingers wrapped briefly around his.

Shaken by the strength of the feeling welling up in her, Mallory made a small movement of withdrawal. It was an instinctive, not conscious, action. David sensed her pulling back instantly, and although he wanted to hold on to her, he released her hand.

Mallory took a deep breath, calling on her considerable reserves of poise. "I'm . . . I'm glad to meet you, Dr. Hitchcock," she said after a second.

Surprise flickered through his eyes. "Doctor?" he repeated. "Did I leave my stethoscope on? Or did the smell of disinfectant give me away?"

She liked his sense of humor. "Well, actually, I asked the man at the meat counter who you were," she confessed.

"Ah. I'm flattered. And you're—?"

Mallory hesitated. While David apparently hadn't recognized her face, she was afraid her name might ring a bell. "I'm Mallory Victor," she said, taking the plunge.

"Mallory Victor." He repeated her name as though he enjoyed the sound of it. "Are you new to Farmington, Ms. Victor?"

"Mallory, please."

"David, then. Not Doctor."

"David."

"Are you new to town?" he asked again.

Mallory touched her hair, the unabashed interest in his eyes flustering her slightly. "I've been here for about two weeks. I'm staying at a friend's place."

"Oh." He tried not to think about the possibility— the likelihood, given her looks and style—that the friend was a man. "Are you on vacation, then?"

Mallory hesitated, debating her answer. "Sort of," she said finally, opting for a partial truth rather than an outright deception. "I'm . . . taking some time off from my work."

He nodded, wondering if she was having problems coming to terms with her husband's death. He could see hints of stress in her dark eyes, and she was definitely on the underweight side of thin.

"Are you from Farmington?" she asked him. She was genuinely curious about his background. She was also aware that as long as he was answering her questions, she wouldn't have to answer his.

"Born and raised here."

"It's a beautiful town," she remarked sincerely, a sparkle coming into her dark eyes. "I like New England a lot. There's such a sense of . . . oh, history and stability." Of all the places she'd traveled on tour in the past ten years, New England had always held a special attraction. When she'd told her manager, Bernie McGillis, that she had to get away, she'd mentioned New England longingly. He, through some undisclosed maneuvering, had come up with a condominium in Farmington, Connecticut.

"Are you from this part of the country?"

Mallory felt as though she'd been from nowhere and everywhere during the past decade—for longer than that really. But she didn't want to explain about that . . . not yet.

"I was born in the Midwest. Ohio. I have a place in California now." It was in the hills outside Los Angeles. She and Bobby had bought it three years before. They'd only spent about six months in it. Much of what they—

she—owned was still in packing crates.

"L.A.?" he inquired.

"It's that obvious?" she parried lightly. She'd made a special effort to fit in here in Farmington, doing her best to adopt what she considered a protective suburban coloration.

"Lucky guess."

They'd started to wheel their carts down the aisle, moving together in companionable rhythm. "Didn't you want a pineapple?" Mallory asked after a brief but comfortable silence.

"I hate pineapple," he said with a grin. "But it seemed like a good way to start a conversation."

Mallory laughed, pushing her cart around the corner and heading toward the check-out counters. She heard the implied confession of attraction in his words with a sense of womanly pleasure. His candor drew her like a lodestone. "I was thinking about dumping a pile of cans in your path," she confided.

"Why?"

"I wanted you to notice me."

His grin became a smile of masculine appreciation. "You don't need cans to accomplish that," he assured her frankly. His blue-gray eyes eloquently informed her that he had, indeed, noticed her . . . and more.

Mallory felt herself flush a little at the compliment, relishing the difference between it and the more practiced come-ons she was used to. She was smiling her response as she joined one of the check-out lines.

It was waiting for her in a wire newspaper rack: a black and white time bomb that exploded in her consciousness like a burst of silent agony.

She saw the huge-eyed, grainy picture of her face first, staring out from the front page of a nationally known tabloid. Then she read the banner headline:

Molly V Mystery: Having Bobby's Baby?

Mallory swayed, the blood draining from her cheeks. Nausea clawed at her stomach. She clutched at the slick metal push bar of her cart, fighting a sickening wave of dizziness.

David saw the change come over her with a surge of alarm that went far beyond professional concern or brief personal acquaintanceship. He had no idea what had triggered the reaction. He only knew that she'd been smiling one moment and was pale and shaken the next. She looked like a woman caught unaware by a nightmare.

He moved to her swiftly, reaching out to steady her. Their bodies touched intimately for a few seconds, hers as boneless as a rag doll's, his rock-steady and comforting.

"Mallory?" he questioned, his eyes very intent and assessing. With instinctive professionalism, he brought one hand up, deftly seeking the pulse point at the side of her throat. It beat out a rapid, pounding rhythm beneath his fingers.

Struggling to maintain her equilibrium, Mallory sucked in a shuddery breath and passed the back of her right hand tremblingly over her forehead. As she did so, her sleeve pulled back, baring her inner wrist. There, on the pale skin, was the delicate but distinctly tattooed image of an angel.

"Mallory?" David repeated, too concerned about what was happening to her to give more than fleeting consideration to the unusual mark he saw on her right wrist. He couldn't make out what it was. Slowly, he removed his hand from her neck.

"I'm—all right," she said as firmly as she could. The urge to lean against him, to draw on what she sensed was his bedrock of emotional and physical strength, was almost irresistible, but she did not give in to it. It wouldn't be fair to him. And it wouldn't be right for her—not now, not when she was trying to put her life back together for herself, by herself.

David's eyes were full of questions, but he refrained from asking them. He also held back from trying to hold on to her when he felt her pull back. His arms felt empty when he let go of her.

"Are you sure you're okay?" he asked, trying to force his mind into a professional track. Lord, every fiber of his body seemed imprinted with the feel and fit of her. His nostrils were full of the evocative fragrance of her skin and hair.

Mallory nodded, inhaling deeply, then summoned up a small but determined smile. She breathed a silent word of thanks that David apparently had not noticed the tabloid cover. She suspected he was the kind of person who barely registered the existence of such publications.

She registered them, though. Dear God, how she registered them!

"Mallory?" he probed again. There was a gutsiness in her smile that touched him deeply. Mallory Victor was plainly a woman of unexpected strengths... and, he sensed, undisclosed scars.

"I'm fine," she said, her smile becoming less fixed and more genuine. "I was just woozy for a minute." She straightened her shoulders.

"Have you had dizzy spells before?" He was relieved to see some color creeping back into her cheeks.

Mallory shrugged with studied casualness and positioned her cart alongside the check-out counter. "I'm all right, really," she said. "I–I skipped lunch and that probably made me a little lightheaded." She began to unpack her groceries.

David could easily believe that she had missed lunch— and a considerable number of other meals besides—but he doubted that an empty stomach accounted for her dizziness. She'd been frightened as well. What in the world could have made her react that way?

Mallory could sense his curiosity and concern and she wanted to deflect them... at least for now. Although instinct told her she could trust this man, experience had made her extremely cautious about opening up to people. She wanted to know David Hitchcock better—she *would* know him better—and then, maybe then, she would tell him the truth about herself . . . Bobby . . . and the angel on her wrist.

"Don't worry, Dr. Hitchcock," she said, injecting a teasing note into her voice and taking special pains to emphasize his professional title. "I'm okay."

It wasn't exactly a brush-off, but David had an unpleasant suspicion it might turn into one if he pushed her. The last thing in the world he wanted was to lose this woman before he had a chance to know her . . . to touch her . . .

"Okay," he nodded, giving her a reassuring grin. Unable to stop himself, he reached out and brushed her cheek gently with the knuckles of two fingers. Her skin *was* as exquisitely soft as it looked. He promised himself he'd judge the sweetness of her mouth before much more time had passed.

The tenderness of his touch unnerved her. It made her recall, once again, how long it had been since she'd been with a man.

"Doctor?" Despite her best efforts, a flirtatious huskiness had crept into her voice.

"David," he corrected firmly, watching the sparkle dancing deep in her brown eyes. "I'm sorry if I came on too strong. Chalk it up to my professional training."

The sparkle in her eyes became distinctly sassy. "You had professional training in coming on?" she inquired dulcetly.

David laughed. "Oh, sure. It was a required course in med school," he returned.

Mallory joined in his laughter, thankful that the awkwardness of the moment had been smoothed over.

They exited the store about ten minutes later, pushing carts filled with bagged groceries. The blustery wind was brisk and bone-chillingly cold and there was about a foot of snow on the ground. Although the supermarket parking lot had been well plowed, the pavement was still very slick, and Mallory had to pick her path gingerly due to the fashionably high heels of her boots. Bobby had bought the boots for her from an exclusive shop on Beverly Hills' Rodeo Drive, and she adored the sleek length they added to her legs. She was beginning to realize, however, that what worked in L.A.'s untroubled climate was not so practical in New England.

"Easy," David counseled, gripping her forearm in a lightning-fast reflex as she nearly lost her balance on a deceptive, snow-dusted patch of ice.

"Thanks," she said breathlessly, steadying herself with a palm against his chest. The wind whipped her dark hair with invisible fingers and brought a rosy color to her cheeks. "I'm a notorious klutz," she joked.

"That I seriously doubt." His eyes ran over her in a swift, encompassing glance and he smiled at her with the certainty of a man who had tracked her blood-stirringly graceful movements up and down the aisles of the supermarket.

Mallory felt the touch of his eyes and gave a tiny shiver that had nothing to do with the cold. The color in her cheeks deepened and warmed. "You don't believe me?"

"No. Oh, you may be notorious. But a klutz? Never."

"Thanks for the vote of confidence." She wondered at his casual repetition of the word *notorious*. Did he suspect something? Or was he just teasing?

How would Dr. David Hitchcock react if—when— he found out who Mallory Victor really was?

David watched the changeable emotions flickering across her provocative face for several seconds, caught once again by her appealing combination of vulnerability and strength. Who was she . . . really? he asked himself, thoroughly captivated by this intriguing, tantalizing puzzle of a woman.

"My pleasure, Mallory," he returned finally, investing the words with a caressing quality that set a deeply responsive chord vibrating within her.

Suddenly shy, Mallory dropped her long lashes, veiling her eyes. Her heart gave a curious flutter. She felt excited yet uncertain...and full of a strangely sweet sense of anticipation.

"Um...this is my car," she said, taking refuge in the prosaic as she wheeled her cart up beside an eminently serviceable gray Ford sedan. It was a rental. Her manager had arranged for her to get something much flashier, but she'd asked for a more discreet vehicle. Mallory had no desire to call any unnecessary attention to herself.

David helped her load her groceries into the trunk, lifting and positioning the heavily packed bags with characteristic dexterity and precision.

"Thank you," Mallory told him, tilting her chin slightly to smile up into his eyes. Deep inside the pockets of her down jacket, her hands clenched as she fought down the sudden urge to brush back the strands of brown-blond hair that had blown across his forehead.

"You're welcome," he replied.

There was a silence on both sides. Their eyes locked in an exchange of messages neither one of them was quite ready to voice.

"Have dinner with me tomorrow night?" David invited at last. "Unless you have plans?" he tacked on, recalling her mention of a friend's place.

"No plans," she replied honestly. Plans were something Mallory had been avoiding. Until now she'd been content to spend her time in Farmington reading, listening to music, puttering in the kitchen, and noodling on the well-tuned, upright piano in the condo's living room. She suspected Bernie had arranged for the piano. It didn't quite fit with the stark, contemporary style of the rest of the place.

"Then—?"

"Yes," she said simply, "I'd love to have dinner with you tomorrow night."

- 2 -

"Bernie—" Mallory began, exasperated, trying unsuccessfully to stem the flood of words gushing out of the phone into her ear. Standing in her stocking feet, clad only in an ivory silk charmeuse slip, she was attempting to juggle the phone with one hand and go through the contents of her closet with the other. She was about ready to give up on her wardrobe—and her manager.

"Molly, just listen to me. This is a terrific deal—"

"Bernie, *no!*" she interrupted emphatically, wishing for the zillionth time that her manager wouldn't call her Molly. "I'm not going to do a poster posed in lingerie. I'm—what?"

"I said this isn't just any lingerie. It's that French designer stuff you like so much."

Mallory rolled her eyes. She'd always had a weakness for slinky, sophisticated lingerie. Unfortunately, the

19

weakness had been so exploited in building up her image as *Molly V, sexy rock star* that she was about ready to discard silk and lace for cotton T-shirts and boxer shorts.

"Look, I don't care if it's got my name monogrammed on it," she informed her manager. "It doesn't matter whether it's mass-produced by Frederick's of Hollywood or handmade by nuns in some Spanish convent. I am *not* going to do the poster. No. Nyet. Never. *No way!*"

Gnawing on the knuckle of her right index finger, Mallory tuned out the verbal explosion this statement touched off. She stared disgustedly into the closet. She'd been trying on and taking off clothes for the better part of an hour in preparation for her date with David. The growing pile of rejects flung on the bed and the floor testified as to how little luck she was having finding something—anything!—to wear.

Lord, *what* had been going through her head when she'd packed for Connecticut? Actually, "packed" probably wasn't the right word. She'd simply gone into her closet in the Los Angeles house, scooped up about a half dozen armsful of clothing, and dumped them into a pair of suitcases.

Oh, she'd brought plenty of pairs of custom-tailored jeans and an adequate selection of easy but expensive tops, but that wasn't what she was looking for tonight. There were several brightly patterned summer dresses, too, as well as a black leather miniskirt and matching jacket, two hand-knit pullover sweaters from Italy, a gorgeous Bob Mackie beaded dress she'd gotten for the Grammy Awards two years before, a mind-boggling assortment of uncoordinated coordinates, and a liberal sampling of the antique and "junk shop" fashions she'd picked up over the years. None of these outfits seemed right, either. To Mallory's critical eye, everything she'd brought with her screamed either rock-and-roll or weirdo—or both.

Neither of those labels was likely to appeal to Dr.

David Hitchcock. And she wanted very much to appeal to him.

"Molly, are you hearing me on this?"

Bernie's irritated inquiry jerked her out of contemplating her clothes. "Yes, I'm hearing you, Bernie," she said wryly. "Considering that you're yelling, I can hardly help it."

"Babe, I'm trying to help you. You've had your career on hold for months now. I know the last Fallen Angel album's still hot, but you—Molly V—are going to cool off if you don't get some exposure soon."

"'Exposure' as in this poster?"

"Exactly," he said emphatically, apparently oblivious to her sarcasm. "Look, I'm really trying to be understanding, but you're making it very hard. First, you tell me not to negotiate a new recording contract even though I've got at least four top labels drooling offers on my desk. Then you pull some kind of weird withdrawal stunt and just sit around while Fallen Angel falls apart and Colin Swann picks up the pieces. Are you nuts? How could you let yourself be dumped by the best back-up band in the business?"

"To begin with, Bernie, they didn't *dump* me. They're professional musicians and they want to work. I couldn't ask them to sit around doing nothing while I was making up my mind about what I want to do with my life."

"So you let Swann—"

"Don't try to paint him as the villain. You know as well as I do that that last album would never have been finished if Colin hadn't stepped in when Bobby died."

"Maybe," Bernie grunted. "But now he's formed Nightshade and has Coney, Rick, and Boomer with him on tour. Where does that leave you?"

"In Connecticut," she snapped.

"Get serious, babe. You've worked too damned hard to get where you are to toss it away with this kind of flaky behavior."

There was a pause.

"Molly?" Bernie prodded.

"Mmm?" Mallory squinted her eyes at a flashy, multihued silk blouse she didn't think she'd ever worn. She wasn't about to break that pattern tonight!

"Are you on something?"

"Wha—*no!*" Mallory stared into the receiver. As Bernie well knew, she had never touched—or been tempted by—drugs. In fact, she seldom took aspirin. In the weeks immediately following Bobby's death, when she'd been struggling to finish that star-crossed final album—it was called "Tumble to Earth"—she'd been offered everything from prescription sleeping pills to high-quality cocaine. She'd always said no.

"Are you sure?" Bernie demanded.

"Yes, I'm sure," she returned angrily. "You know me better than that."

"I'm beginning to wonder if I know you at all. You used to be so easy to work with."

"You mean, I used to do everything you told me to do."

"Are you accusing me of mismanaging you?"

Mallory knew the outrage in Bernie's voice was genuine, and she felt a pang of regret. The problem was with her, not with him. Bernie McGillis wasn't a Boy Scout, but he was basically honest and unquestionably hardworking.

"No, of course not," she said. "I'm not accusing you of anything. I just need some time to myself, that's all. I told you that when you arranged this place for me."

"Honey, you're tying my hands! Look, how am I supposed to do my job if you won't give me a hint of what you want?"

"Bernie, the only thing I want at this point is for you to hang up so I can figure out what I'm going to wear tonight," she said. She began sorting through the closet again. No . . . definitely not . . . yuck . . . well, *maybe*—

"What's tonight?" Bernie demanded sharply.

Mallory hesitated, mentally chiding herself for opening the subject. "I'm going out tonight," she admitted finally.

"Out? As in with a guy?"

"Yes."

"Who is he?"

Mallory closed her eyes for a moment, trying to shut out the image of Bernie's PR machine swinging into action. "None of your business," she replied. She kept her tone mild in an effort to take the edge off her refusal to answer.

"Everything you do is my business."

"No, everything Molly V does is your business." It was literally true. Since signing on as her—and Fallen Angel's—manager, Bernie McGillis had overseen virtually every facet of her life. He'd even selected the dress she'd worn for her marriage to Bobby five years before. Mallory's secret yearning had been for something traditional. Bernie had convinced her that white leather with silver beads and fur trim was more in keeping with her image. Deep down, Mallory still winced at her wedding pictures.

"Molly," Bernie began, adopting a patient, long-suffering voice. "Molly, babe, I've got your best interests at heart. If you're getting involved with somebody—"

"Bernie! I'd hardly call having dinner—"

"What about what could happen *after* dinner? I mean, if a guy goes out with Molly V—"

"He doesn't know who I am."

"What? Who does he think you are? Shirley Temple?"

Mallory fingered a silver silk jumpsuit, shaking her head. "He knows my name is Mallory Victor. He—I haven't said anything about Molly V."

There was a certain amount of distaste in the way she said "Molly V." Molly V was Mallory's alter ego—her protective, professional coloration. Molly was the one who handled the press with a snappy comeback or a sultry smile. She was the one who kept tens of thousands of screaming fans satisfied with her songs and sexy strut.

Molly kept Mallory sane. She also drove her crazy.

"He didn't recognize you?"

"No." Thank God, she added tacitly.

"Doesn't that tell you something about what you're doing to your career?" her manager demanded.

Mallory had to laugh. "What it tells me is that there are still some people in the world who don't listen to rock-and-roll and read sleazy tabloids. Besides, without my makeup and all the rest of the glitz, I look like a normal person."

"Normal!" Bernie spat out the word as though it tasted bad. "Who wants to look like a 'normal person'?"

"I do," Mallory answered simply. "Especially tonight. So, if you'll let me hang up—" She broke off, catching sight of something tucked away in the corner of the closet. "Perfect!" she exclaimed, pulling the garment out. "This is just what I want."

"This" was a calf-length tobacco brown velvet skirt. Suddenly inspired, she reached into the closet again and took out a creamy pale Victorian-style blouse. It was high-necked with an intricate, lace-inset yoke. Wedging the phone between her shoulder and jaw, Mallory held both garments to her chin and glanced at the full-length mirror on the inside of the closet door.

"That's more like it," she murmured with a pleased smile. With her boots and a belt, she'd look just right.

"Molly," said a tinny voice in her ear. She ignored it.

Well, *almost* just right. She was going to have to wear her fur coat. Bobby had given her the sable six years ago when Fallen Angel's second album had gone platinum. It had been a profligate, impulsive, and typically Bobby gesture. The endearing boyishness of his generosity had kept Mallory from protesting his extravagance—or mentioning her philosophic objections to fur coats. She'd worn the garment enough times to please Bobby, but she'd never really felt comfortable in it.

Still, given that the only other outer wrap she'd brought with her was the yellow down jacket, she supposed she'd have to go with the fur.

"Molly—"

"Bernie, I've got to run. Bye. Thanks for calling."

And, in an unprecedented move, Mallory hung up on her manager.

"David, this is lovely," Mallory said about forty minutes later as they settled into an intimate corner table in the restaurant he'd chosen for their first dinner together.

He smiled at her, pleased by her reaction. This restaurant was one of his favorites, and he'd hoped she'd share his appreciation of it. Of course, what he'd really wanted to do tonight was to invite Mallory home with him, make her one of his fail-safe omelets (or heat up one of his housekeeper's frozen gourmet delights), and get to know her in private...

Get to know her. David felt his body stirring in response to the idea, and warned himself to take this one step at a time. He hadn't forgotten the fear and vulnerability he had seen in Mallory the day before.

But, Lord, he wanted to touch her! Everything about her—the glossy tumble of her dark hair, the petal-pale smoothness of her skin, the sensual textures of her clothing—tempted him. She was so damned inviting!

And so damned...intriguing.

"I'm glad you approve," he told her. "You said you like New England. I thought this place might appeal to you."

"Oh, it does," she assured him, flattered that he had remembered her remark in the supermarket.

The restaurant was a converted gristmill. Despite its out-of-the-way location, a quick glance revealed that it was doing a booming business with a well-heeled and discriminating clientele. Mallory had not missed the warm greeting David had gotten when they'd arrived.

The setting was both romantic and restful. The thick gray stone walls and polished oak plank floor lent an aura of restrained, solid elegance. Rich cream and teal blue dominated the color scheme and there were enlivening touches of burgundy and pewter throughout. A fire crackled in the main dining room's huge stone hearth and bayberry candles flickered on each table.

The beautifully hand-lettered menus listed a delectable array of dishes that had nothing to do with trendy culinary tastes and everything to do with the best of American home cooking. After months of having little or no appetite, Mallory found her mouth watering as she read the list of entrées.

"Do you see anything you like?" David asked, a little amused by the greedy way she was poring over the menu.

"Everything!" she said with a little laugh. "I'm starving."

"Did you skip lunch again?"

She looked blank for a moment, then realized he was referring to the excuse she'd given for her dizziness the day before. "Oh, no. I'm just . . . hungry."

"I like a woman who appreciates good food," he commented. There was a faint, flirtatious drawl to the way he spoke.

Mallory's mouth curved up at the corners. "I thought doctors were supposed to lecture people about the dangers of overeating."

"Mmm . . . probably. But, as a man, I have to say I approve of a healthy appetite." The drawl progressed from flirtatious to provocative. "Besides, I don't think you have to worry about overeating."

Her lips parted on a responsive smile, revealing the tiny chip that marred an otherwise even line of white teeth. "Thank you—I think," she replied.

"Don't think. It was a compliment. And you're welcome." Lifting his water glass, he toasted her. "To a healthy appetite, Ms. Victor."

Flushing slightly, she lifted her own glass. "To a healthy appetite, Dr. Hitchcock."

Then Mallory relaxed, enjoying David's easy charm and an absolutely delicious meal. It had been a long time since she'd had an evening like this.

"You never did tell me what kind of work you do," David remarked casually, nodding his thanks to the waiter who had just refilled their water glasses.

"Didn't I?" Mallory parried, forking up the last bite of glazed butternut squash that had come with her roast chicken and cornbread stuffing.

He shook his head. "Yesterday at the supermarket, you simply mentioned that you were taking some time off."

Mallory stalled for a moment, toying with her fork. "I write music," she said finally. "And I . . . sing."

"Ah." There was something . . . artistic . . . about her. And there was no denying the musical huskiness of her voice. "Was your husband a musician?"

"Y–yes. That's how we met."

The answer was essentially accurate but basically evasive. Mallory didn't want to lie to David, but she wasn't ready to open up to him, either. Barriers that had taken years to go up did not crumble overnight.

David sensed her reticence and respected it . . . and yet—he wanted to know about her . . . all about her.

He took a sip of his wine. "I know this is probably the worst thing to admit at this point," he commented with a rueful smile. "But I'm not . . . familiar . . . with your work."

"That's all right. I don't think it would be your kind of thing, anyway."

"Pop music?"

"Mmm." She accepted his categorization without blinking. The other members of Fallen Angel would have swallowed their respective instruments whole before they'd tolerate the label. Molly V and her group played rock-and-roll.

"I strike you as that far out of it?"

"What? Oh, no. No, of course not," she assured him hastily. While she had no doubt that David Hitchcock preferred Haydn to heavy metal, she didn't want him to think she held that against him.

David grinned at her. Behind the glasses, his eyes were warm and teasing. "It's okay, Mallory. Thanks to Lori, I'm well aware that I'm not exactly with it."

"Lori?"

"My sister. Half sister, if you want to be precise. My mother died when I was fourteen. My father remarried a couple of years later. A year after that, Lori was born. She's sixteen now."

"And very much with it?" Mallory guessed.

"She likes to think she is," he conceded with equal parts affection and exasperation. "She's basically a good kid. She does tend to act and talk before she thinks, but I suppose that's part of being sixteen. Still, it would save a lot of grief if she'd at least pause before she—oh, say—dyed her hair pink."

"She dyed her hair *pink?*" Given David's quietly upper-class appearance—the fine gray herringbone suit, the white broadcloth shirt, the maroon foulard silk tie, the thin wristwatch and monogrammed, silver cuff links —she would have imagined that the women of his family were charter members of the preppy set. "But why?"

"Good question. Adolescent rebellion, I guess. My stepmother does a lot of charity work. Lori went public with her new hair color the day her mother was hostess of a tea party for one of her most important committees."

"I see." Mallory could envision the scene.

"Fortunately, the dye job was temporary. Otherwise, I think my father would have shaved her head."

"She really would have been with it then."

"I beg your pardon?"

"Bald women are very fashionable in some circles," Mallory explained with a mischievous twinkle.

Unable to restrain himself, David reached across the table and brushed her mink-dark curls. "I hope you don't travel in those circles," he told her softly.

Instinctively, Mallory turned her face into the warm curve of his fingers. His palm shaped the line of her cheek for a long, heady moment. Mesmerized by the seductiveness of the contact, Mallory brought her right hand up and lightly stroked his knuckles. As she did so, the cuff of her sleeve pulled back slightly, revealing part of her distinctive angel tattoo. Beneath the fine cotton of her blouse and the sleek silk of her slip, her breasts tautened with yearning. She felt herself trembling on the brink of some momentous discovery.

"David—"

"Mallory—"

"Excuse me, sir. Are you done?" Their waiter suddenly materialized by the table. His tone was politely helpful.

Forcing himself to swallow a surge of frustration, David withdrew his hand. Part of him wanted to dismiss the waiter in no uncertain terms. Fortunately, his innate courtesy prevailed.

"Yes, I'm finished," he said. "Thank you." Picking up his linen napkin, he pressed it against his mouth. He could smell Mallory's scent on his fingertips.

Mallory had dropped her hand into her lap, self-consciously smoothing the velvet folds of her skirt. She felt both embarrassed and exhilarated.

"Miss?"

She looked at the waiter. "Yes?"

"Are you finished?"

"Oh—yes, I am. Thank you."

The waiter cleared their places deftly, apparently oblivious to the strained silence that had fallen between his two customers. After what seemed like an interminable amount of fussing, he took their dessert orders and bustled away.

Don't hurry back, David thought.

Mallory drank some of her wine. "Did you always want to be a doctor?" she asked after a moment, thinking about her own youthful ambitions . . . and how hard she'd worked to fulfill them.

David moved his wine glass in a circle. "I always had an affinity for medicine," he said slowly, "but I decided to become a doctor when I was fourteen."

"Fourteen." She hesitated for a few seconds. "You said . . . that was when your mother—?"

"Yes," he replied without elaboration. His devotion to medicine was inextricably linked to his mother's untimely—her *unnecessary*—death. But it was not something he spoke about easily.

"It must be rewarding—being a doctor," she said softly.

"I can't imagine myself being anything else," he answered honestly.

"The man in the supermarket said something about your getting a Presidential award for your work?" She wondered fleetingly if David might be irritated by her curiosity. After all, she didn't like people prying into her life. Perhaps he—?

"The man at the supermarket?"

"The one at the meat counter. I asked him your name—"

"Oh, yes." He smiled. "Well, the White House citation was for a medical outreach clinic in Hartford. But it's not fair to call it 'my work.' I was only one of a large group of people who helped get it off the ground."

"You must have done *something* special," she insisted. She liked his refusal to grab all the credit for himself. Genuine modesty—like a great many other genuine things—was in extremely short supply in the entertainment world. She knew a lot of people in the music business who took bows every time it thundered.

"I did what I could. Along with plenty of other people. Including my stepmother, Liz."

"Oh?"

"Well, most of her causes are a bit more fashionable—"

"Fashionable?"

"Sure. The Gala Against Gallstones—"

Mallory laughed. "You made that up!"

"A slight exaggeration. In any case, Liz plied enough people with cocktails and canapés to get the contributions we needed to get the project started. Nowadays, a fundraiser with her ability is as valuable as a fairy godmother."

"Mmm." Mallory made a mental note to have Bernie look into the possibility of her making an anonymous donation to the clinic.

"Speaking of fairy godmothers—" he said, deciding to direct the conversation back to her. "Do you mind if I ask you something personal?"

He saw a hint of wariness appear in her brown eyes, muting their brightness like a shadowy windowshade.

"You can ask," she replied cautiously.

But you won't necessarily answer, David tacked on silently.

"I was wondering about the wings on your wrist," he said after a fractional pause.

"Wings?" She looked at him blankly, momentarily thrown by the unexpected direction of the inquiry.

"On your right wrist," he amended. "I saw the mark yesterday when you rubbed your head in the supermarket. And again tonight—"

Mallory fought down a panicky urge to cover her wrist with her hand. To anyone who knew the rock world, the tattoo was a dead giveaway. To someone without such knowledge . . .

"Oh, you mean my tattoo," she said, striving for a casual tone.

"Your tattoo?"

She nodded. "A . . . souvenir of my ill-spent youth," she explained, still trying to sound offhand. All the members of Fallen Angel had had angel tattoos when she'd first joined Bobby on the road. Mallory had gotten one herself primarily out of a desire to fit in. She'd wanted—needed—to belong.

"It's—what? A bird?" David wondered if the tattoo reminded her of something she'd prefer to forget. Tattoos had a way of doing that. He still recalled an emergency room patient he'd treated during his internship. The man, a bridegroom-to-be, had been the victim of an ill-fated effort to have an elaborate tattoo removed from his chest. The tattoo had pledged eternal love to someone named Matilda. The man's fiancée was Suzanne.

"It's an angel," she told him softly.

He responded with a slow, teasing smile. "Is it supposed to be you?" he asked. An angel would suit her, he thought.

Mallory dropped her eyes, feeling her cheeks grow warm. "I . . . I've been accused of being a lot of things," she said reflectively, and for a fleeting moment her expression took on a melancholy cast, "but an angel isn't one of them."

"This really was wonderful," Mallory told David sincerely about an hour later as he held her chair while she rose from the table.

"I'm glad you enjoyed it. But we don't have to leave yet, you know. There's still time to get another serving of dessert."

Mallory laughed and shook her head. She'd devoured hers—a delicious concoction of hot apple cobbler and homemade cinnamon ice cream—with what she considered almost embarrassing enthusiasm. But, somehow, the contrasting sweet-spicy tastes and the play of the cold ice cream against the hot fruit had seemed too sensuously tempting to resist. In the back of her mind, she realized that the sudden restoration of her appetite had as much to do with David's company as it did with the excellent food.

"Are you sure?" he asked tantalizingly.

"Unless you want to roll me into your car like a giant beach ball, I don't think—David?" She felt him stiffen slightly behind her. Half turning to look at him, she saw that his attention had been caught by something happening a few tables away.

A middle-aged man was coughing, his face a plum-red. As Mallory watched, he tried to take a sputtering gulp of water, but it didn't seem to help. His dinner companion, an elegant older woman, began to pat him on the back, her expression revealing a mounting alarm.

What happened next took only about ninety seconds. Afterward, however, Mallory found she could replay each instant with crystalline clarity, like a perfectly shot slow-motion film.

David brushed by her and moved to the table in four lithe strides. By this time, a waiter had hurried over and several nearby patrons had risen to see what was going on. David waved everyone back with a quick, compelling gesture. They responded wordlessly to the purposeful-ness in his manner.

He said something, low and steady, as he got the gasping man from his seat. Mallory couldn't make out the words, but the tone was both assuring and authori-tative. Eyes wide, she watched as David positioned him-self behind the man and wrapped his arms around him in what—as she vaguely recalled from a late night public service announcement—was called the "hug of life."

Making a fist with one hand, David placed it carefully

above the man's navel but below his rib cage. Using his other hand for leverage, he pulled in and up in a smooth, sure movement.

Whatever the man was choking on dislodged. After a moment, he drew a shuddering, gulping breath.

It was only then that Mallory realized the dining room had fallen silent as this life-and-death drama played itself out. The man half collapsed into his seat, and the place exploded into conversation, laced—amazingly—with a smattering of applause.

Mallory took several steps toward David, her impulse to try to do something to help. He seemed to sense her nearness because he glanced at her, then he fished in his pocket and pulled out his car keys. He tossed them to her.

"Can you get my bag?" he asked. "It's in the back seat."

She nodded and turned.

By the time she got back, flushed and a little out of breath because she'd run most the way, David, the choking man, and the woman with him had been moved into the antique-furnished office of the restaurant's manager.

"Thank you," David said as Mallory put the bag down beside him. The two words were abrupt, but the fleeting smile of appreciation that flashed across his face warmed her.

"Is my husband going to be all right?" the woman asked, staring at David in anxious, hopeful supplication.

"Nora, I'm all right," the man told her. Except for a slight shakiness in his voice, he seemed almost completely recovered. "Thanks to the doctor here, I'm all right."

"He is fine, Mrs. Lawrence," David said calmly, opening his leather medical bag. The woman had introduced herself and her husband once they got to the manager's office. "It was a frightening experience, I know, but there's no permanent damage."

"But John could have——" Mrs. Lawrence began, a stricken look in her eyes. "If you hadn't been here——"

Mallory recognized that the woman was just starting to realize the gravity of what had nearly transpired. Instinctively, she crossed to her and touched her shoulder. "But David was here, Mrs. Lawrence. And it's all right now. Really."

It took David ten minutes to give John Lawrence a clean bill of health. The restaurant manager came in and out several times during those ten minutes, pale with relief that a potential tragedy had been averted, but obviously troubled about the restaurant's liability in the episode.

He stopped them at the exit as they were finally on their way out, half an hour later. The Lawrences had already gone.

"I——ah——hope this hasn't ruined your evening, Dr. Hitchcock," he said.

David shook his head as he finished assisting Mallory into her fur coat. "Not at all. I'm glad I was here to help."

"Yes, indeed," the manager agreed with a nervous bob of his head. "Your dinner is on the house, of course."

"That isn't necessary," said David.

The manager gestured. "But we'd like to show our appreciation——"

"It isn't necessary," David repeated.

"Surely, there's *something*——" the other man insisted.

David ran his hand back through his hair. "The best way you can show your appreciation is to make sure that your staff gets some training in first aid," he said smiling. "The local Y has a good course. So does the Red Cross."

"First aid," the manager echoed. "That's an excellent idea. Well . . . I hope you'll be back."

David slipped his arm around Mallory's waist and gave her a warm smile. "I think we will," he replied.

She smiled back.

* * *

It was nearing midnight when David pulled up before the condominium where Mallory was staying. He parked beside a street lamp. Its soft glow illuminated the interior of the car. It frosted the dark cloud of Mallory's hair with silver and underscored the gamine quality of her face.

"So," David said, undoing his seat belt and turning toward her.

"So," she echoed, undoing her seat belt and shifting to face him.

They studied each other in measured silence for several moments. Questioning . . . wondering . . .

Mallory fluffed her curls with one hand. All her senses were heightened. The events of this evening had brought David into dynamic, dangerously attractive focus for her. She could feel herself beginning to go limp. A strange sense of shyness and an instinctive flirtatiousness prompted her to veil her brown eyes with her lashes.

David tracked the artless but unmistakably sensual movement of her fingers. His gaze then slipped to her faintly parted lips . . . the same soft lips he had been savoring in his imagination for the past twenty-four hours.

Mallory felt the touch of his eyes like a kiss and her mouth curved into a small, very feminine smile. After a few seconds, she raised her lids to look at him.

She hesitated for just a moment. Aside from thanking her for her help, David had resolutely steered their conversation away from the incident in the restaurant ever since they'd gotten into the car. While she thought she understood his attitude, she still felt the need to voice her admiration for what he had done.

"You know," she said slowly, deciding to try the light approach, "if you planned that episode with Mr. Lawrence to impress me, it worked." She hesitated again. "I . . . it was great! You saved that man's life!"

"I'm a doctor," he said simply, barely conscious that

he had invested the last word with a strong charge of emotion.

She nodded, sensing the dedication in the way he spoke. "Still, to be able . . . aren't you happy?"

"Sure! I'm glad I was there, glad I was able to help," he said. "But, right here, right now . . ." He gave her a slow, crooked grin. "Don't ask me why, but I'm suddenly feeling like I'm back in high school."

The implicit admission of uncertainty surprised her for a moment. But the honesty of his words touched her because she thought she understood what he was trying to say. The sexual chemistry between them—right here, right now—was an unnerving as it was intensely exciting. While she was scarcely an inexperienced girl, there was something new . . . something unfamiliar . . . about what she was feeling.

She cleared her throat. "You mean . . . you're wondering how far I'm going to let you go on the first date?"

He chuckled deep in his throat, feeling more in tune with her than he ever had with a woman in his life. "To tell the truth, Mallory," he replied, his voice dropping as he leaned forward to stroke the side of her face, "I'm wondering how far I'm going to let myself go."

Mallory moistened her lips with a flick of her tongue . . . waiting.

The gray in his eyes turned to molten silver. "I suppose there's only one way to find out, isn't there?" he asked and drew her to him.

It was a kiss of slow, heated sweetness . . . intoxicating as mulled wine. David's lips closed over hers with a hungry tenderness that provoked and promised, fueling the honeyed urgency that surged through her responsive body.

It was a kiss of adult desire, yet it held a hint of innocence. There was an enchanting, evocative freshness to this caress: the offering of new and fruitful beginnings. It was a kiss of testing . . . and trusting.

The flavor and feel of her mouth were all David had imagined and more. Her lips moved tantalizingly beneath his, parting in answer to the gentle, probing demand of his tongue, then opening fully to invite a deeper possession.

Mallory's hands slid up the length of his arms, moved across the strong breadth of his shoulders, and linked behind his neck. Her slender fingers delved into the springy-crisp thicket of hair growing at his nape. The clean male scent of him filled her nostrils like a rare perfume. She inhaled it deeply—and with pleasure.

He traced the velvety inner circle of her mouth with arousing languor, then found the chipped edge of her front tooth with the tip of his tongue. She answered his explorations with a shudder of pleasure and a throaty purr.

She shuddered again as David kissed a swift, searing trail to her ear. The shadowy stubble of his new beard growth rasped her skin with erotic friction, sending tiny prickles of excitement darting through her bloodstream like fireflies. She sucked in her breath as she felt him catch the vulnerable flesh of her earlobe between his teeth.

"Da—vid!"

He licked the place he had just nibbled on, teasing the outer curve of her ear with his tongue. "Sweet," he murmured huskily. "So . . . sweet."

After months of emptiness and indifference, Mallory felt herself blossoming with a warmth and wanting that was the essence of life. She'd endured the cold darkness of solitude for so long, it was a shock to step out into the sunlight of intimacy again.

The shock made her bold. Turning her head, she sought and found David's mouth. She nipped teasingly at his lower lip, tempting him with a darting flutter of her tongue.

David groaned and gathered her closer. She was affecting him like a potent, mainlined drug—electrifying his senses, setting fire to his nervous system. He wanted to bury himself within her. To know her utterly . . . completely.

Even through the separating barriers of their winter clothing, Mallory was aware of the fierce power of his arousal. She gloried in the feel of his masculine strength, shifting against him.

She was lost in him. Blinded to place, unaware of the passage of time, she felt herself being swept beyond conventional boundaries.

David wanted this woman with a hunger and a possessiveness that was new to him. He needed her. Ached for her. He was a scrupulous, caring man. A deeply honorable and dedicated man who had ordered his life into strict priorities. But the urgency of his desire at this moment made him heedless of circumstances and careless of consequences. He was ready to have her right here, right now—

HONK!

- *3* -

AFTERWARD, DAVID TOLD HIMSELF—none too persuasively—that he would have come to his senses even if his elbow *hadn't* made heavy contact with the steering wheel. As it was, the honk of his car horn jolted him into a sudden awareness of just exactly where he was and just exactly what he was on the verge of doing. He let go of Mallory, trying to ignore the heated clamoring of his body.

Mallory sat up. Her hands shook as she made a hasty effort to straighten her carefully chosen clothes and pat her hair back into order. Dear Lord, what was happening to her? David had touched her, kissed her, and she'd gone up like a Fourth of July fireworks display! Mallory was far from an innocent or a prude, but she'd never responded to *anyone*—not even Bobby—with such abandon.

David shifted, mentally berating himself for his lack

of control. He sucked in a deep breath.

"Mallory—" he began. His voice was not quite steady. He cleared his throat. "Mallory, I'm sorry," he said.

She looked at him incredulously. Her wide eyes shimmered with vulnerability and her kiss-bruised mouth trembled. It was all David could do not to take her in his arms again.

He was sorry? For what? she asked herself. Her heart was fluttering like a trapped butterfly.

David's sandy-brown hair had been tousled by her fingers and his glasses were slightly askew. Without thinking, Mallory impulsively reached out to straighten them.

David forestalled her by removing his glasses entirely. His self-restraint was stretched as tight as an overworked rubber band, and it would take very little to snap it. To have her touch him again—

"The lenses are fogged up," he said, groaning inwardly at the lameness of the attempted explanation. Fogged up lenses? Hell, the whole inside of the car had been fogged!

Mallory pulled her hand back. Her blood was pulsing through her veins in an irregular rhythm.

David shoved his glasses into his coat pocket. "Mallory, I am sorry," he repeated. He raked his strong, capable hands back through his hair, mussing it even further. "I wanted this evening to be special for both of us. I wanted us to have a chance to get to know each other. So, what do I do? I jump on you like some—some adolescent stud. I'm a thirty-six-year-old man, for Pete's sake!"

Right, Hitchcock, a sardonic little voice inside his head piped up. And since when have thirty-six-year-old men been immune to sexy women?

Mallory bit her lip, searching for a way to defuse the tension. "Well," she said slowly, "you *did* say you felt like you were back in high school." It was the kind of teasing remark she often tossed at the guys in the band. For a moment, she wasn't quite certain how David would take it.

Questioning blue-gray eyes met lambently demure brown ones. Everything stood still for a few breathless, silent seconds. Then, by some mysterious alchemy, awkwardness dissolved into humor.

"Feeling like I'm back in high school is one thing," he replied, his mouth quirking into a self-mocking smile. *"Acting* like it is something else."

"It certainly is." The response was definitely sassy. After a second or so, Mallory started to laugh at the absurdity of the situation. She tried to dam up the bubbling mirth with her hands, but it spilled out of her like champagne foaming from a shaken bottle.

David began laughing, too. The open, honest quality of the sound touched Mallory as deeply, as seductively, as anything else he'd done that night.

"O—okay," David finally gasped. "What's so funny?"

"I—" Mallory hiccuped. "I don't know."

"Then why are you laughing?"

"I don't—for the same reason you are."

"Do you have any idea what that might be?" he was still chuckling a little.

Mallory shook her head. "No."

He grinned. "Good. I'd hate to think you know something I don't."

Mallory smiled back.

He shook his head, growing a bit more serious. "God, necking in a parked car," he said as though he still didn't believe it. He looked over at Mallory. "I . . . don't usually act that way," he assured her.

Too bad, she thought, remembering the erotic search of his firm mouth over hers. Having David act "that way" was one of the best things that had ever happened to her. Still, she supposed she could understand his embarrassment.

"I—I don't usually act like that, either," she said, twisting a thick lock of hair around one finger. Her eyes darted away from his craggily attractive face for a moment, then returned, drawn like iron filings to a magnet. "Did you . . . were you what you said before? When you were a teenager?"

It took him a moment to realize what she was asking.

"Was I an—ah—'adolescent stud'?" He reflected on his high school years with a mixture of nostalgia and loathing. As they did for many people, those days lived in his memory as the best of times . . . and the worst. "I was adolescent, yes. As for the other: I guess I had aspirations in that direction from time to time, but I was at an all-boys' prep school." He grinned wryly. "I'll bet you were the belle of the ball when you were younger."

"You'd lose," she told him simply. "I wasn't even invited to the prom." After all this time, the thought still rankled. Even if she had been invited, her foster parents probably wouldn't have allowed her to go. They hadn't approved of Mallory wasting her time on boys anymore than they had approved of her enthusiasm for rock music.

"If that's the case, I'd say the boys who went to your prom were the losers," David said flatly.

Mallory had been on the receiving end of a great deal of glib flattery from a great many glib men during the past ten years. She seldom let it touch her. David's backhanded little compliment slipped right through her guard. "Thank you," she said sincerely, feeling the lingering hurt of the dateless prom night fade.

"My pleasure."

Silence filled the car. It lasted for the space of two . . . three . . . four heartbeats.

"Well," Mallory said at last, trying to fight off an awareness that she was perfectly willing to go on sitting in the car with him for the rest of the night. "Well, I think I'd better go in."

"I'll walk you—"

"No, that's all right." Her dark hair moved silkenly around the pale oval of her face as she shook her head.

"But—"

"I know the way." She smiled to soften her refusal. Then, leaning forward, she brushed a feathery kiss against his mouth. "This evening was very special to me, Dr. Hitchcock."

"It was special for me, too," he responded, running the tip of one finger tenderly down the curve of her cheek. "Would you consider doing this again? Having dinner with me, I mean." He withdrew his hand and gestured around the car. "Not the—ah—rest."

Mallory opened the door and got out before she answered. Feeling a little lightheaded, she bent to look at him. "Yes, I'd consider having dinner with you again," she confirmed softly, and very carefully shut the door.

She'd consider having lunch and breakfast with him, too. In fact, given the slightest hint of encouragement, she knew she'd consider doing "the rest" with him again as well.

Two weeks later, Mallory stood in a clearing in David's two-acre wooded backyard, laughingly preparing to test her hand and eye coordination against his.

The match-up had not been on their original agenda. When David had invited her to spend this Saturday with him, he'd also requested her help in picking out some presents for his half sister's upcoming birthday. The plan had been that they would have an early lunch at his place, go shopping afterward, then play the rest of the day by ear.

It had been a good plan—especially, Mallory had thought, the playing it by ear part. Unfortunately, the lure of the sun sparkling on a fresh new blanket of snow had tempted them into a tramp around David's property. That had led to the construction of a decidedly malformed snowman, followed by a fierce snowball fight in which

David's superior aim was offset by Mallory's surprisingly sneaky tactics.

Neither side had been willing to concede defeat in the battle, so David eventually proposed settling the issue by a contest of skill. After Mallory consented to the idea, he'd collected five of the largest pine cones she'd ever seen and carefully arranged them in a row on a log. He then proceeded to invent a list of rules that would have confused Howard Cosell.

"So, we're agreed?" he asked with a grin. "Best out of five snowballs wins."

Mallory pretended to consider this while she painstakingly formed a snowball with her orange mittened hands. The mittens probably were a little garish, she reflected. Especially since she was wearing them with her yellow down jacket, a green wool scarf, and a peacock blue knit hat. Still, the flamboyant combination suited her cheerful mood.

"Mallory?"

She smiled at him. Her blossoming beauty made him catch his breath. There was a rosy bloom in her cheeks and a bewitching sparkle in her dark eyes. The haunted quality he had seen in her the first time they'd met had all but vanished and she'd put on a few pounds in some becoming places.

"What happens if there's a tie?" she asked him.

His tawny brows went up. "In the event of a tie, the decision of the judge is final."

"Ah." Bending down, she placed the snowball on the ground beside the other ones she had made. She flipped her scarf back over her shoulder as she straightened. "And who, pray tell, is the judge?" She cocked her head inquiringly.

He folded his arms across his chest. "Me."

"You?"

"Uh-huh. It's my land."

"Oh-ho." She chuckled mockingly. "And I suppose if

I don't play by your rules, you'll take all your snowballs and go home?"

"Could be." His even teeth flashed white against his tanned skin as he grinned again. The outdoors—clear, crisp, and clean—suited him very well, Mallory decided, drinking in the healthy male virility of him. David Hitchcock was quite at ease with his surroundings. She'd learned that he enjoyed sailing and cross-country skiing in his spare time. Judging by the athletic economy of his movements and his aura of assured self-sufficiency, Mallory suspected he was very good at both.

"You know, I don't think this is going to be a fair contest," she complained. "You should have a handicap."

"Hey, I'm not wearing my glasses, remember?" He'd taken them off and pocketed them when they'd begun building their snowman. Mallory had decided he looked a little younger and a bit less intellectual without them. She'd also noticed that he had very long, thick eyelashes. "What more of a handicap do you want? I can barely see the target!"

"You didn't seem to have any trouble finding the target during our snowball fight," she reminded him.

"Yes, well, you're not an easy person to miss, Ms. Victor. Especially when you're decked out like a box of crayons."

She gave him an indignant glare. "I resent that remark, Dr. Hitchcock. What's wrong with the way I'm decked out?"

"Not a thing," he assured her, laughing. For all his teasing, David thought Mallory looked extremely appealing—like some exotic bird or butterfly. Her kaleidoscopic appearance was in keeping with what he'd discovered was her sometimes mercurial personality. "But you have to admit you don't exactly blend in with your surroundings."

A shadowy uncertainty passed over Mallory's face. During the past two weeks, she'd become less uptight about what she wore when she was around David. Had she loosened up too much?

David saw the uncertainty and realized that he'd un-intentionally struck a nerve. Damn! The last thing in the world he wanted to do was hurt this woman. But there were still so many things he didn't fully understand about her. So many hidden sensitivities, so many unanswered questions—

"I'm not trying to blend in." She could hardly change her outfit at this point. Besides, she liked the way she looked!

"No?"

"No. I wore all these colors to make sure no hunter mistook me for a deer or something." She deliberately emphasized the light retort with a "so there" smile.

"I see."

"I also wanted to make sure that if we got lost, the searchers could spot us." She looked at him critically, taking in his boots, gray corduroy pants, and slate parka. "They'd never find you, you know," she remarked.

"True," he agreed solemnly. "But we are not going to get lost because one, I was an Eagle Scout; two, I know these woods like the back of my hand; and three—"

"You left a trail of breadcrumbs from your house?" she suggested brightly.

He gave her a quelling look. "Shall we get back to the snowball contest?"

She shrugged in mock-resignation. "Oh, very well. Best out of five wins."

"Right."

Mallory picked up one of her snowballs. "Wins what?" she asked.

David scooped up a fluffy handful of snow and began packing it into the proper form. "Wins what?" he par-roted.

Mallory grimaced. "What does the best out of five win?" she elaborated.

"Oh." He considered for a moment, a provocative gleam suddenly appearing in his gray-blue eyes. "Best out of five wins a forfeit from the loser," he declared with dangerous simplicity.

"A . . . forfeit?" Her heart gave a curious skip as she realized his gaze had moved to her mouth. She and David had kissed and touched each time they'd been together during the past two weeks, of course, but always with a conscious restraint. Mallory knew David wanted her, but she sensed he was as wary as she was about plunging into a physical relationship.

At least he seemed to be . . .

She had no doubt that taking the plunge would be intensely pleasurable for both of them. It was the thought of what might come afterward that troubled her.

At least it had seemed to trouble her . . .

"A forfeit," David repeated with quiet but deliberate emphasis. Their eyes met for a long, breathless second. "Winner's choice."

David won. While Mallory managed to knock four pine cones cleanly off the log, he got all five thanks to a ricochet.

"Unfair," Mallory protested. "This was supposed to be a test of skill."

"I got two pine cones with one snowball. What could be more skillful than that?"

"You were lucky."

"True," he conceded. "But being lucky is a skill."

"David—" Mallory wondered why she was objecting. She knew perfectly well what forfeit he was going to claim. And she knew perfectly well she wasn't going to mind yielding to that claim.

"You play, you pay."

"Did you have to memorize that to become an Eagle Scout?"

"No, I learned it in a floating poker game at prep school."

"Ah." She moistened her lips with the tip of her tongue, her mind flashing back over the lyrics of an old rock song called "Anticipation." "You really think we should count your ricochet?"

"Nothing in the rules against it."

She laughed. Somehow during the past minute or so, they'd gotten within touching distance. "Yes, but you made up the rules," she pointed out.

"Next time *you* can make up the rules."

"Is there going to be a next time?"

"That depends."

"On what?" They were only about six inches apart now. The white-bright sunshine glinted off the gold in his wind-tousled hair. Looking up at him, Mallory could see the fine lines radiating out from the corners of his eyes—lines of living, laughter, and caring. She had a sudden desire to trace the whitened scar on the jut of his chin with her fingertips. She wanted to memorize the disciplined sensuality of his mouth, too.

"On whether or not you're going to pay the forfeit," he said softly. The wildflower sexiness of her perfume teased his nostrils like a tantalizing hint of spring warmth in the winter coldness.

She smiled. "I play, I pay," she answered, her voice equally soft.

There was a small pause. David's blue-gray eyes darkened to a navy-slate.

"Aren't you going to ask what the forfeit is?" he inquired.

"I think I've got a pretty good idea." Her own eyes had gone wide and soft. In their dark depths was the message that whatever forfeit he chose to claim, it would only be a prelude to what she would freely give him.

"Do you?" For a crazy split-second, David wondered if making love in the snow would lead to frostbite. Maybe they could generate enough body heat—?

"Uh-huh."

"Well—" He ran one finger slowly up the zippered front of her down jacket. As bulky as the garment was, there was no doubting the femininity of the body wearing it. "I *had* considered demanding your scarf..."

"My scarf?"

"It would come in handy if I ever got lost in the woods. On the other hand, your hat—" His hand moved upward and pulled off the blue knit cap. Most of Mallory's hair had been tucked up beneath it. The dark curls tumbled down around her face in riotous freedom. Mallory trembled a little as he toyed with several of the silken ringlets. His fingers teased the sensitive lobe of her left ear, marking the tiger's eye stud and the gleaming gold hoop she wore there.

"You...want me to forfeit my h–hat?" Her voice was hushed and breathy.

He shook his head. "No. I want you to forfeit a kiss."

Mallory didn't so much hear him say "kiss" as she *felt* it spiral through her nervous system. David's mouth closed over hers even before he finished speaking the word.

His lips were firm, seeking, heatedly male. Hers were soft, yielding, welcomingly feminine. There was a moment of melting tenderness, followed by a heady rush of mutual hunger.

Mallory pressed against him, her movements sinuous and supple. She invited the search of his tongue and responded with an erotic little thrust of her own.

She enticed...appealed. She shifted her body, fitting her slender delicacy to his hard strength. She offered... aroused...

David savored the sweetness of her mouth. Sipping. Sucking. Courting and conquering with leisurely, lingering expertise. He kissed her cheeks, her chin, the lids of her eyes...then returned to claim her moist, quivering lips once again.

Mallory made a sound of instinctive protest when he

lifted his head. He gazed down at her hungrily, wanting to memorize each detail of her face. Her cheeks were flushed to a heated pink and her pupils were huge in her dark eyes. She looked exquisitely desirable and vibrantly alive.

"Mallory—" Her name came out in a silvery cloud of condensation. The sound evaporated with the mist but the underlying passion in it hung in the air. "Mallory, let's go inside."

She nodded once, and he took her hand in his.

Inside, the telephone was ringing. Mallory had the feeling it had been ringing for some time.

David gave her a ruefully apologetic smile as he picked up the receiver. His blue-gray eyes promised that whatever it was, it would not take long. Mallory nodded her comprehension. A few more minutes...

"Hello?" His voice was level and polite but his hands weren't quite steady as he began to unsnap his parka. "Yes, this is Dr. Hitchcock."

Mallory caught her breath as she saw him stiffen in response to what was being said on the other end. Even before he spoke again, she knew it was going to be far more than a few minutes before they would be able to finish what they had begun outside in the woods. Angry, frustrated disappointment lanced through her.

"Yes, I understand," David was saying. His features had gone grim. The mobile, sensual mouth that had caressed and kissed her so tenderly only minutes before thinned. "Right away. Thank you for calling me—what? Yes, please. Tell them." He dropped the phone back into its receiver and turned to face Mallory.

"A patient?" she asked, peeling off her orange mittens and stuffing them into the pocket of her jacket.

He nodded. "An emergency."

"I'm sorry."

"So am I," he responded in an odd tone. He knew

what he had to do; he'd done it countless times before. Yet, suddenly, he genuinely, consciously *resented* the demands of the profession to which he had dedicated himself thoroughly. Devotion to medicine—to healing the sick and comforting the hurt—was the cornerstone of his life. But at this moment, staring at Mallory, he felt that cornerstone shift.

The feeling shook him . . . to his very core.

"Look, Mallory," he said, "I've got to go to the hospital. I don't know that there's anything I can do at this point, but the family is asking for me—"

"I understand," she said immediately. She did understand why he had to leave. David's commitment to his work was something she admired and respected. What she did *not* understand was why he was looking at her so intently.

"I hate to run out—"

"Don't apologize," she cut in swiftly, taking a step forward and placing a gentle palm against his cheek. "Go. I'll—I'll be here when you get back."

He looked surprised. "I have no idea how long this will take," he told her frankly.

"I'd like to wait." The initial pledge had come out of her spontaneously, but she realized she meant it sincerely. "If—if you don't mind, that is."

For a moment, the grimness disappeared from his face. His mind embraced and cherished the idea of having Mallory waiting for him when he came back from whatever he was going to have to face at the hospital. "I don't mind at all," he said softly.

"You're sure?"

"Positive." Dipping his head, he brushed a brief but stirring kiss across her faintly parted lips. "Make yourself at home. I *will* be back."

It felt a little strange being alone in David's house. Strange, yet oddly right. Mallory had felt like a transient in the world since her parents' deaths. She knew, instinctively, that this was a place a person could settle . . . put down roots.

She hung up her yellow down jacket and the rest of her outdoor things on the gleaming brass coat rack sitting next to the front door. After a moment, she removed her boots, wiggling her toes against the slightly worn but still beautiful Oriental rug on the polished wooden floor. She peeled off the black angora sweater she had put on over a full-sleeved rose silk shirt and sleek blue denim jeans and hung it up, too.

David had given her a brief tour of the downstairs part of his house when she'd arrived. It consisted of a surprisingly modern kitchen, a rather formal dining room that smelled faintly of lemony wood polish, a handsomely appointed living room, and an obviously much-used and slightly untidy den. The furnishings throughout were in quiet, classic good taste, with natural materials and earth tones predominating. The basic look was English-American; the overall impression was one of unpretentious comfort combined with understated elegance.

There were no decorator touches, no calculatedly trendy gimmicks. It had a distinctly masculine air, yet it was a far cry from the plush, proverbial bachelor's pad.

She liked the house. And she liked the man who lived here. In fact, she could imagine herself—

Yes, a mocking little voice whispered suddenly. But can you imagine Molly V?

Shaking off these thoughts, Mallory wandered into the den. She glanced longingly at the stack of wood and kindling arranged in the hearth of the fireplace that dominated one wall. All it needed was a match . . .

Later, she decided. When David comes . . . home.

The room's built-in, floor-to-ceiling bookshelves—crammed with everything from a battered high school biology text to a beautifully bound first edition of J. J.

Audubon's *Birds of America,* from an eclectic selection
of mystery novels to a well-thumbed assortment of sailing
manuals—yielded plenty of reading material for her wait.
A quick survey of David's extensive record collection
turned up recordings of some familiar classical pieces as
well as four Beatles' albums and three by the Beach Boys.

She was curled up in a brown leather chair in the
corner of the room, soothed to sleepiness by the fluid
magic of Handel's "Water Music," when the doorbell
chimed. The sound jerked her upright, shattering the
daydreams she had been weaving and leaving her momentarily disoriented.

"Where—?"

The bell rang again.

"Uh—" Mallory got to her feet, brushing her hair out
of her face. "Uh—just a minute!" she called.

She opened the ebony front door a few moments later
and came face to face with a petite, pixie-pretty teenager.
The girl seemed as surprised to see her as she was to see
the girl.

"Uh—hi," the teenager said, studying her with big
blue eyes. She had a porcelain complexion and short,
curly blond hair. "I'm Lori Hitchcock. Is my brother
here?"

Mallory shook her head, suddenly wishing she'd taken
the time to put her boots back on. "I'm afraid not," she
replied. "He's out on an emergency call."

"*That* figures," Lori responded, slumping. "Rats."
She dragged the last word out with a funny grimace. "Is
he going to be gone long?"

"I don't know."

"Can I wait around?"

"I—" Mallory surrendered to the beseechingly hopeful
expression on Lori's face. "Of course. Come in. My
name is Mallory, by the way. I'm a friend of David's."

"Glad to meet you," Lori replied, coming inside. She
casually shucked off her jacket and, after a glance at

Mallory's bare feet, unselfconsciously kicked off her shoes. "I hate shoes," she informed Mallory with a conspiratorial smile.

Mallory smiled back. "I won't tell if you don't."

Lori laughed. "Okay—uh, Mallory, right?"

"Right."

There was a moment of silence. Then Lori's fair, unplucked brows came together in a troubled expression. "Have I met you before?" she asked with youthful directness.

Mallory's stomach knotted. She knew that look—that "I-know-the-face-but-I-can't-quite-place-it" look—all too well.

"No, we've never met," she said.

"Oh . . ."

"Would you like something to eat, Lori?" Mallory improvised quickly. "I was about to fix myself a salad."

The mention of food distracted the pretty teenager. Her face cleared. "Oh, sure, thanks. That'd be nice."

Lori trailed Mallory into the kitchen, chattering artlessly the whole time. She was a friendly, confiding girl who obviously liked to talk.

"Of course, it's probably going to be ages before David gets back," she observed, standing on tiptoe to reach a teak salad bowl on an upper cabinet shelf. She set it down on the tiled kitchen counter with a *thunk*. "He gets really wrapped up in his patients. But I guess you probably know that already, huh? Being his friend, I mean."

"Mmm," Mallory nodded, opening the refrigerator.

"I think it's 'cause of his mother," Lori went on consideringly. "Like maybe he's trying to make up for that other doctor's mistake."

Mallory's head came up. She couldn't hide her surprise. "Mistake?"

"Uh-oh." Guilty distress clouded Lori's blue eyes. "I—you didn't know about that?"

"David told me . . . he said he decided to become a

doctor the same year his mother died," Mallory replied slowly. She'd felt there had to be more to the timing of that decision than he'd said, but she hadn't imagined something like this. "But I didn't realize—"

"He doesn't talk about it much," Lori said. "He holds things in, you know. I don't know the whole story. But I guess his mother got sick and the doctor she went to didn't diagnose it right. When they finally found out what was really wrong..." her voice trailed off.

Mallory nodded slowly.

"Um..." Lori was chewing her lower lip. "You won't tell David I said anything, will you? I mean, it's not a big secret, but he doesn't like people talking about him. Like I said, he's really private about some things."

"I won't say anything," Mallory agreed.

"Whew." The teenager smiled gratefully and levered herself up to sit on top of the counter. "David's always getting on me about having a big mouth," she confessed.

Mallory slid open the vegetable crisper drawer and took out the ingredients for their salad. "Do you have a big mouth?" she inquired lightly. A part of her wanted Lori to go on talking about David. Ethically, however, she shied at the idea of pumping a sixteen-year-old for information.

Lori made a funny face, recovering her good spirits. "Yeah, probably," she admitted. She swung her leg back and forth for a few moments. "My dad says I have a big mouth, too. He—we had a fight this morning. That's why I came here. I wanted to talk to David."

Mallory brought the vegetables she'd selected to the sink. She began rolling up the cuffs of her silk shirt. "Does he take your side in things?"

"Are you kidding?" Lori giggled. "David's worse than my dad sometimes! The weird thing is, though, even when he tells me the same stuff my parents do, it seems to make more sense coming from him."

"I see." In a strange way, Mallory thought she did.

She envied Lori her obvious closeness with David. She turned on the water to rinse the salad ingredients.

"Yeah, he's a pretty neat guy," Lori declared. "In fact, I think—"

"You think what?" Mallory prompted, glancing at the girl.

"Ohmigod!" Lori said in a hushed little voice. Her eyes were fixed on the tattooed angel on Mallory's right wrist.

- 4 -

MALLORY'S HEART sank.

"I *knew* I knew you! You're her!" Lori hopped off the counter and did an excited little jig. "You're Molly V!"

For a moment, Mallory considered denying everything, but the expression on Lori's young face told her such a ploy probably wouldn't work. Besides, Mallory had never been a very good liar. She could omit or evade the truth if she had to, but she had no real talent for out-and-out deception.

"Yes," she said reluctantly. "I'm Molly V."

Lori clapped her hands together. "Oh, wow! I can't believe this—this is *amazing!* I have all your albums. I love your music. Especially your last record, 'Tumble to Earth.'" She gave a breathy laugh. "Molly V... here. In Farmington. And you—you're making me *lunch!*"

"Even superstars have to eat," Mallory countered wryly,

trying to put a damper on Lori's volatility. She was human enough to be flattered by the teenager's enthusiasm, but she didn't want the girl to get carried away.

"Well, but—" Lori's look implied that stars of Mallory's magnitude should be dining on caviar and champagne, not salad.

"Besides, Mallory Victor is making you lunch."

"What?" Lori looked uncertain.

"Molly V is who I am on stage. Here—making you lunch—I'm Mallory Victor."

"Oh." Lori took a moment to adjust to this. "You mean like you're—uh, what's that word? Oh, yeah. *Incognito*. You mean like you're here incognito?"

"Mallory Victor *is* my real name—"

"Yeah, but—" Lori broke off, her eyes going huge with astonishment and accusation as a new thought struck her. "David never said anything. I didn't even know he *knew* you!"

An icy knot formed in Mallory's stomach. "He . . . David doesn't know he knows Molly V."

"Huh?" The single syllable came out blunt and bewildered. Mallory wondered if she'd been as easy to read at sixteen; she didn't think so. Four unhappy years in foster care had taught her to keep her feelings to herself.

"Look, Lori," she began, not quite certain how she could explain to a teenager she'd just met what she could barely explain to herself at this point. "I'm here in Farmington taking a . . . a break. I—the past year was pretty rough."

"Because—because of your husband?" Lori had stopped dancing around. "And—uh—Fallen Angel breaking up and stuff?"

Mallory sighed, realizing she probably should have expected such questions. If Lori was as enthusiastic a fan as she seemed to be, she no doubt knew all about Bobby Donovan's death and its scandal-tinged aftermath.

"That's part of it," she confirmed after a moment.

"And I suppose you could say I'm here incognito—at least for a while."

"You mean David *really* doesn't know who you are?" Lori's skeptical tone suggested this was on par to not knowing who was the President of the United States.

"He really doesn't know," Mallory answered. "He knows me as Mallory Victor, a woman he met in Farmington, Connecticut. He has no idea I'm Molly V."

"I don't see how he can't," Lori protested. "You're famous!" She made a sweeping gesture to underscore her point. "All my friends know who you are."

Mallory tried not to smile at the girl's simplistic view of the world. "I'd imagine that's because all your friends like rock music. But if your brother's record collection is anything to go by, I don't think he fits into that category."

"Well, yeah, I guess . . ."

"I'll bet he wouldn't know a Molly V song if he heard one."

"Oh, yes, he would," Lori contradicted emphatically. It was unclear whether she was trying to protect her half brother against a charge of ignorance or to reassure Mallory about her popularity as a performer. "I stayed with him last summer while my parents were on vacation and I played your albums all the time. David wanted to know what they were because he said the noise was driving him—uh—" She went beet red. "Never mind."

"He said it drove him nuts?" Mallory finished mildly.

"I used to play the albums really loud," Lori rushed to explain. "And David was working hard—"

Mallory touched her shoulder reassuringly. "It's all right."

"He mostly likes classical music," Lori added apologetically. She shifted awkwardly, not meeting Mallory's eyes.

"It's *all right*, Lori. I understand."

The teenager looked at her warily. "You aren't mad?"

"No. I've been criticized for a lot worse things than driving people nuts with my music."

"Well..." Lori still didn't seem totally sure that she hadn't bruised Mallory's ego. There was a moment of silence. Then her chagrined expression gave way to a look of dawning mischief. "Boy, is David going to be embarrassed. Just wait till I tell him!"

Mallory caught her breath. "I–I wish you wouldn't, Lori."

The teenager blinked, visibly thrown. "Why not?"

"I...just wish you wouldn't."

Lori frowned. "You want to tell him yourself?"

Mallory nodded slowly. "Yes, I want to tell David myself. But I want to do it at the right time...in the right way."

There was a pause. "Are you worried about him blabbing to people?" the teenager finally asked, her forehead wrinkling.

"No, not at all." The denial was quick and sincere. "I *am* going to tell him," she repeated. "But I want David to know me better before I do. It's...people usually react very strangely to me because I'm Molly V. My image gets in the way of them treating me like a real person. Remember—even you were surprised that I was making you lunch."

"Yeah," Lori conceded thoughtfully. "So, like, you want to be sure he likes you for yourself and not because you're a big rock star?"

"Well—"

"I mean, I guess a lot of guys probably fall for you just because you're Molly V, right? The only thing is, David isn't like that. Really, Mol—I mean, Mallory."

"I know he isn't." Mallory paused, searching for the right words. She finally settled for the unvarnished truth about why she was keeping her identity a secret. "Lori, I'm not worried about David being turned on by the fact that I'm Molly V. I'm worried that he might be turned *off*."

It took Lori a good thirty seconds to digest this notion. "You think he might freak out or something?"

"Something like that," Mallory agreed. "But you know him better than I do. What do you think?"

Lori bit her lower lip. "Well . . . I guess . . . maybe . . ." Her obvious reluctance to answer was an answer in itself.

"Never mind." Mallory put an end to the girl's struggle with a shake of her head. "It was wrong of me to put you on the spot by asking you that. In fact—" she sighed. "In fact, I shouldn't have put you on the spot by asking you to lie to David—"

"You didn't ask me to lie," Lori jumped in, her troubled expression turning into a conspiratorial smile. "You just don't want me telling the whole truth. And it's okay. Actually, it's going to be kind of neat knowing something David doesn't know." She giggled. "A whole new experience for me. Of course, I may have to tape my mouth shut to keep from spilling the beans." She slanted Mallory a wistfully hopeful, faintly wheedling look. "I—uh—guess I can't tell my friends about you, can I?"

The corners of Mallory's mouth quirked up. "I don't think that's a very good idea," she confirmed.

"Yeah, probably not. Anyway, they'd never believe me. I mean, Molly V in *Farmington?*"

"You say that as though Farmington is the end of the world."

"Well, compared with most of the places you've been—"

"Compared with most of the places I've been, Farmington's wonderful."

"You don't think it's boring?"

Mallory smiled. She could hear—and understand—the yearning for excitement in Lori's voice. "Boring is spending eighteen hours straight in a stuffy studio trying to get the vocal track of a song right," she said. "It's necessary, but it's boring."

"Yeah, but going on tour! Flying around in a jet, partying—"

"Bus," Mallory corrected.

"What?"

"When I go on tour, I go by bus. And when you do two hundred plus one-night stands in two hundred plus days, you don't have much time for partying."

Memories assailed her. Touring had been anything but boring in the early hand-to-mouth days when Fallen Angel had gone around in a secondhand van, existing on a budget that made eating three meals a day an impossible luxury. And there had been something wildly, almost uncontrollably thrilling about touring in the wake of Fallen Angel's first, chartbusting success. But after ten years . . .

"You—you're not going to quit, are you?" Lori asked.

What, and give up show biz? Mallory thought, mentally invoking the punchline of an ancient joke involving a man who cleaned up after circus elephants.

"I'm not sure what I'm going to do," she told David's half sister after a few seconds.

"Well, you can't quit. You're so good!"

"Thanks. But I don't even have a band anymore."

"Oh . . . yeah. Rick, Boomer, and Coney—they're all in Nightshade now, huh? With Colin Swann." Lori giggled, her blue eyes sparkling. "I bet *he's* not boring. I think he's a hunk!"

"So do a lot of other women."

Lori cocked her head. "Are you and Colin . . . I mean, I read in some magazine—?"

Mallory's expression became serious. "You can't believe most of what you read, Lori."

David came home shortly before seven that evening. Lori had left hours before, her stomach full of three servings of salad and her mind stuffed with Mallory's stories about the real world of rock-and-roll. The teenager repeated her pledge of silence as she was saying good-bye. She also dropped a rather unsubtle hint about Nightshade's upcoming concert appearance in Hartford. Laughing, Mallory promised to see about getting the girl some complimentary tickets—and perhaps even a pair of backstage passes.

Mallory was in the kitchen when she heard the front door open. She'd been luxuriating in the tranquillity of the house, mentally replaying the scene in the snow and indulging in a small fantasy about what it would be like to live in this place . . . with David.

He was hanging up his parka when she reached the front hall.

"David?" she said softly.

He turned. His attractive, asymmetrical features held equal parts exhaustion and exhilaration. The weariness eased as he offered her a slow smile of infinite warmth. Mallory responded to it with one of her own; her heart skipped a beat, lanced by a feeling of tenderness she had never experienced before.

"You waited." Until that moment, he hadn't allowed himself to realize how much he'd been counting on finding her here when he returned. David had always shouldered the burdens of his profession alone. Yet, suddenly, the idea of being able to share them . . .

"I said I would," she told him. She wanted to erase the lines in his forehead and relax the tension she read in his lean body. "Is the patient—?"

"He's alive. He isn't out of the woods yet, but the indications are favorable."

"I'm glad," Mallory said.

"So am I." The steady simplicity of the three words held a wealth of carefully controlled emotion.

To David, it seemed like the most natural thing in the world to open his arms to Mallory at that moment. To her, it seemed like the most natural thing in the world to go to him and to melt into the welcome of his embrace.

There was nothing overtly sexual about the way he held her, yet the press of their bodies was infinitely intimate. He slid his warm palms around her slender waist, marveling at the supple strength of her body as he stroked her spine through the fine fabric of her blouse. The top of her dark head came up to his chin, her silken curls tickling the underside of his firm jaw.

"There wasn't a lot I could do," he said. His voice was low and reflective, coming from deep within his chest. "He was in surgery for five hours. All I could really do is wait along with his family."

"I guess they needed to have you there." Mallory turned her cheek, resting it against the luxurious knit of his gray cashmere pullover. She could hear the steady beat of his heart. "They must have been terrified. And having someone you can trust . . . at a time like that, when your whole world seems to be falling apart—" She took a deep breath, trying not to remember the nightmare that had followed Bobby's death. "It can make all the difference," she concluded with feeling.

"I hope so."

After a moment of silence, Mallory pulled back a little, tilting her head so she could look at his face. "Do you want something—food, maybe?"

The circle of his arms loosened. His chest moved as he filled his lungs with air . . . then slowly let it out. "I ate at the hospital. At least I think I remember eating. I could do with a stiff drink, though. I've got a bottle of Scotch in the kitchen—"

"You go into the den and sit down. I'll fix you the drink. Ice?"

He let her go. "A couple of cubes and a splash of water. Thanks, Mallory."

It took her a few minutes to fix his drink. She collected some crackers and cheese as well before joining him in the den. When she entered, she found him sitting on the floor in front of the fireplace, leaning against several cushions he'd removed from one of the room's sofas. A freshly lit fire was just crackling to life.

"I wanted to do this all day," Mallory commented, handing him the drink. Their fingers brushed and she felt a tiny thrill of excitement dart up her arm. She sank down onto the floor beside him, her long legs folded tailor-fashion. She hadn't thought to put her boots back on. It didn't seem very important at the moment.

David took a swallow of the liquor. "You wanted to do what all day? Have a drink?" He'd slipped off his shoes as well and removed his glasses. His sandy-brown hair was mussed as though he'd run his hands through it several times.

She smiled. "No. Light a fire and sit in front of it."

"Great minds work alike," he replied. He set his glass down on the stone hearth. "But I'm glad you waited."

Their eyes met briefly. Mallory looked away first. David watched as a rosy flush colored her fair face. Her lowered lashes cast crescent shadows on her cheeks. The top two mother-of-pearl buttons of her blouse were undone and he could see the pulse throbbing at the base of her pale, slender throat.

"I hope you didn't find it boring, being here by yourself," he said after a few seconds.

The word boring reminded her of Lori. Shaking her head, she met his gaze again.

"I wasn't at all boring," she said. "In fact, I had a visitor. Your sister Lori stopped by. She wanted to talk to you. Some kind of fight with her parents. I–I don't think it was anything too momentous."

"At sixteen, everything's a crisis." He rubbed the back of his neck with his palm. "I'll call her tomorrow. Did she stay long?"

"About two hours."

"Two hours?" His brows went up. "Do I have any secrets left?"

Mallory laughed again. "A few."

"Do *you* have any secrets left?" His voice was teasing, but there was a hint of seriousness running through it.

"A few," she repeated.

"Hmmm." He was still massaging the nape of his neck.

There was a brief silence, then Mallory volunteered, "I give great back rubs."

He grinned. "If that's an offer, I'll take it."

Beneath the knit of his sweater and the cotton fabric of his shirt, the muscles of his broad shoulders were knotted and tense. At first, it was like trying to dig into rock; there was little or no give. Mallory kept at it, though. She'd unkinked Bobby after hundreds of performances, and her deceptively slender fingers were strong from years of playing the piano and guitar.

The relaxation came gradually. Mallory felt the easing through her fingertips. Instinctively, the massaging movements of her hands became less strenuous and more sensual. David leaned his head forward. He exhaled heavily, a small groan of pleasure coming from deep within his chest.

"Better?" Mallory asked, pressing her knuckles along either side of the top of his spine. She relished this kind of giving physical contact with him.

"Much," he agreed.

"Tension always seems to head right for the back and the shoulders," she observed. His muscles—still taut and toned—were responding more pliantly to her touch now.

"Not always," he murmured, not really meaning to speak aloud. He was aware of a growing tension in the lower portion of his body. The thought of having her hands there—

Mallory felt him shift. "David?" She wondered what he would do if she suggested he might be more comfortable shedding his sweater. The fire was very warm. She was conscious of the heat from it licking at her skin through her silk blouse. She was also conscious of the heat licking underneath her skin . . .

"You have . . . wonderful hands."

She stroked her fingers up into the hair above his nape. Each brown-blond strand seemed to have a thick, springy vitality of its own. "You're the one with wonderful hands," she responded. "I noticed them in the supermarket."

"What did you notice?"

Mallory hesitated for a moment before answering. What she'd noticed had been clues to his character as well as physical power and beauty. "I saw your hands looked strong and capable," she said slowly. "Strong . . . but gentle. The kind of hands a doctor should have." The kind of hands she wanted a man to have.

David turned. The look in his gray-blue eyes reminded her of every touch they'd exchanged over the past two weeks. "I'm not just a doctor, Mallory," he told her with quiet emphasis. He suddenly wanted to make that very clear. It was not a distinction he made often.

"I know that."

He reached forward and touched her face, drawing the tip of his forefinger down the line of her cheek with a tenderness that made her tremble.

"The first thing I noticed about you was your perfume," he said. "It was like the scent of springtime as you walked by: warmth, wildflowers . . . woman." His hand slipped around to cup the back of her head. "All woman. Mine . . ."

He whispered this possessive assertion even as his mouth settled over hers, claiming it in a kiss that began as a teasing, tantalizing caress and swiftly deepened to a heated, hungry search. She yielded, then responded to his demand, her lips opening under his.

He seemed bent on absorbing every nuance of the kiss, relishing the sweetness and the quivering cling of her mouth. He explored and incited with his tongue, evoking the promise of a far more intimate penetration to come.

"I want to make love with you, Mallory," he told her huskily, his mouth nuzzling a leisurely but bloodheating path up the side of her throat. "I want to learn every silken inch of you. I want to go to sleep with the scent of your perfume filling my brain and wake up with the feel of your body warm against mine. Come to bed with me."

She gave her consent with a kiss.

He brought her upstairs to his bedroom, carrying her with a protective care that made her feel deeply cherished. Setting her down almost reluctantly, he flicked a switch that turned on the lamp next to the bed.

"I want to see you," he explained, his eyes sweeping over her. "Do you mind?" He searched her delicate features for hesitation or shyness.

Mallory felt herself flush a little under the intensity of his scrutiny. She shook her head, a soft but unmistakable glow illuminating her dark eyes. "I like the light." There was a provocative note in the voice.

He smiled the slow, crook-cornered smile she had come to know and cherish during the past two weeks. "I want to know everything you like," he said.

They undressed each other with none of the awkwardness of first-time lovers. Their instinctive attunement lent the process an erotic, electric harmony.

Mallory's breath caught at the top of her throat as she took in the tempered, disciplined strength of his naked body. His hair-roughened legs were long and leanly muscled, and there was an athletic power in his calves and thighs. His hips and buttocks were trim; his chest and broad shoulders beautifully proportioned. Her brown eyes tracked down to the proud thrust of his masculine arousal, then moved back to his face. The hunger she saw there made her heart leap.

In turn, David celebrated her nudity with his eyes admiring the exquisite lines of her figure. The pearly sheen of her skin and the beckoning ripeness of her body tempted him at the most basic level.

"You are so beautiful," he told her in a hushed tone, "so very beautiful." And taking her right hand by the wrist, his fingers brushing the angel tattooed on the silken inner skin, he led her to his bed.

Desire clutched at him like a fiery fist as he stretched out beside her, making him realize how achingly deep his need for her went . . . and how fragile his control over that need was. Mallory was warm and willing, but he wanted to wait. He wanted to woo her to completion before taking his pleasure.

He feasted on the bared beauty of her small but full breasts with his eyes and hands. He fondled the firm globes with ardent, arousing appreciation, tracing the outlines of the sensitive nipples with his thumbs. The pink crests peaked in response to his tender, toying attentions, rising like rosebuds in the snow.

Mallory slid her hands up his naked torso, learning the contours of his body as he explored the curves and hollows of hers. Her fingers fanned through the crisp mat of his chest hair, fluttering lightly as they encountered the tight circles of his nipples. She turned her face up slightly, offering her mouth to him.

Her lips parted without urging as he accepted her silent invitation. Her arms circled his neck as he took her tongue into his mouth. The sweet suction of it made her shudder and she clung to him, her slim body shifting in a movement that was agelessly, enticingly feminine.

His hands flowed over her like heated water, warming and sensitizing her skin so that the merest brush of his fingers sent ripples of pleasure running along her nerve endings. She arched in restless, receptive desire as he sought out her most intimate secrets with gentle, skillful hands. He stroked and teased, kindling a fire that raced from the center of her womanhood to the tips of her fingers and toes.

She released a soft, whimpering cry, his name escaping her lips in a shaky exhalation. She whimpered again, unthinkingly digging her nails into him as he quested slowly along the sensitive inner flesh of her upper legs.

"David, please—" she pleaded, her palms coasting up over the muscled firmness of his buttocks and back. "Please—oh, Da—oh!" Her hands clutched at him, fingers splayed, as he caressed once, twice, three times, at the apex of her thighs. Rapture flowered within her, opening like an exotic tropical blossom unfurling its petals.

"Soon," he promised, his eyes flashing quicksilver as he continued to work his sweet, tormenting magic on her body. The feel, the scent, and the sound of her combined to affect him like the most powerful aphrodisiac. The desire to lose himself within her silken heat was almost overwhelming.

"N—now!" she countered frantically, almost past coherent speech. Her newly awakened body seemed sheathed in fire; the flames had to be quenched or they would consume her.

Finally, he shifted up and over her, his mouth swooping down to devour hers with voluptuous hunger as he poised himself for the possession they both desperately wanted. Mallory relished the warm flexibility of his lips. Her hands came up to tangle in his thick, tousled hair. She wanted to envelop him in the same web of sensuality he had so expertly woven about her.

"Yes, Mallory—*now!*" he gritted out and took her in one sure stroke, filling her completely. Her hips rose to meet him and she wrapped her legs around him in a convulsive clasp. She was burningly conscious of the press of her soft breasts against his hard torso and of the seductive tickle of his chest hair against her quivering skin.

For a few moments they were still, teetering on the brink of a pleasure so intense it was like being balanced on the edge of a finely honed knife. Then David began to move within her. Mallory matched his compelling rhythm. As the speed and depth of his thrusts increased, the Earth tilted, tumbling her into a place of star-showered, rainbow-bright sensation. His fingers and lips continued to evoke an erotic litany on her feverishly responsive flesh.

She chanted his name in yearning urgency without even realizing she was doing so. Her eyelids fluttered open suddenly and she looked up into his taut-featured face. He was gazing down at her, watching the eloquently revealing play of expressions on her face with rapt male concentration. For one stunning moment, Mallory thought she could see herself reflected in the blazing depths of his eyes.

A moment later, she was swept beyond rational thought, hurtling into an experience so piercingly sweet, so profoundly elemental, that she was afraid she might faint. David followed her off the brink, groaning his pleasure as he took his own ecstatic release in the shuddering spill of his maleness.

- 5 -

THEY LULLED EACH OTHER to sleep afterward with whispered endearments and soothing, stroking touches. Locked in a lovers' embrace, they drifted off together into sweet, sated oblivion. Mallory dreamed of David.

She thought she was still dreaming many hours later when he began to fondle her again. At first the contact was featherlight, like a warm, tantalizing breeze. Mallory moved in languid, voluptuous response, enjoying the coaxing contact with melting acquiescence.

Just when she realized that she wasn't dreaming, David's hands and mouth became more insistently intimate, and she surfaced into complete consciousness and turned to him.

This time, their lovemaking had the flowing rhythm and the ravishing harmony of a waltz. They merged, then moved as one . . . their pulses throbbing in unison, their breathing coming in ardent counterpoint. They climaxed in the space of the same heartbeat, lips fused, their shared exclamations of pleasure mutually absorbed.

Afterward, they slept again, their arms and legs intertwined. One of David's hands cupped the ripeness of Mallory's left breast as she nestled, unaware, against the protective hardness of his body.

She barely registered it hours later when David stirred her dark tumble of hair off her face and neck and pressed a light, nuzzling kiss against the warm, smooth line of her throat. She murmured—purred, really—at the caress, her soft lips curving into a secret little smile. Underneath the delicate, veined skin of her lids, her eyes moved as if she were dreaming.

Propping himself up on one elbow, David watched her silently for several moments, reviewing the passion of the night before. His body began to harden at the memory of what they'd shared together. He seemed to have absorbed the uniquely arousing feel of her into his cells. The husky sound of her urgent love cries echoed in his brain.

A wave of possessiveness—unfamiliar in its intensity—washed over him as he looked down at her. In the space of two short weeks, this woman had become very special to him. She intrigued and enticed him. He felt he knew her with absolute intimacy in some ways ... and barely at all in others.

He stroked her hair again and she shifted, cuddling against him like a child. Only she was no child. Even lost in the innocence of sleep, she was utterly a woman.

His fingers drifted slowly over the gentle roundness of her shoulder, traced the slim length of her right arm, and ultimately reached the tattoo on her inner wrist. He lingered there for a few seconds, following the artfully done outline of the angel. His expression was thoughtful.

Finally, he kissed her neck again and got up. She turned over as he did so, rolling onto his side of the bed and burying her face in his pillow. The bed linen slipped off the upper half of her body as she moved. After a short but appreciative assessment of what was revealed, he tugged the sheet up and tucked it around her.

Naked, he moved silently about the room, picking up the clothes they had discarded so carelessly the night before. That task done, he donned a pair of well-worn jeans and went downstairs to fix something to eat. He was ravenous.

It was the sense of being alone that first stirred Mallory out of her slumberous state about thirty minutes later. But it was the tantalizing aroma of freshly brewed coffee that brought her fully awake—or at least as awake as she was ever likely to be first thing in the morning.

"Wha—?" she murmured, turning over and levering herself into a sitting position. Brushing her curly tangle of hair out of her face, she blinked. Her sleep-clouded vision cleared and she found herself gazing up at David. He was carrying a heavily laden breakfast tray and he looked devastatingly attractive. His sandy-brown hair was casually mussed and his low-riding, faded jeans hugged his leanly muscled thighs and narrow hips like a second skin.

"Good morning," he said with an amused but affectionate smile. The look in his blue-gray eyes made Mallory disconcertingly but deliciously aware of where she was and how she'd gotten there. Setting the tray on the bedside table, he sat down on the edge of the mattress.

"'ornin'," she said indistinctly, wrapping the sheets around her. Clearing her throat, she tried again. "I mean, good morning."

"I had a feeling you probably were a night bird," he observed. Leaning forward, he brushed a quick but rousing kiss across her faintly parted lips.

"I suppose *you* always get the worm?" she countered. As brief as the kiss had been, it had done a lot to wake her up. There had been many mornings during the past months—too many mornings—when she'd felt reluctant to face another new day. Suddenly she was quite eager to get up and learn what was in store for her.

"Coming awake fast and early is one of the things you learn in the process of becoming a doctor," he told her. "During my internship, I developed a real talent for going from seminaked and semicomatose to fully dressed and totally conscious in thirty seconds flat."

"That sounds like a useful ability to cultivate," she said with rueful humor, thinking back over the countless number of times she'd had to drag her protesting body out of bed for an early morning interview after a hard night on the road. Pushing those memories out of her mind, she glanced at the tray he'd brought upstairs. "Is that breakfast?"

He nodded. "I made it myself."

"You didn't have to." The sudden, embarrassing rumble of her stomach said she was glad he had.

"It's all part of the Hitchcock bedside manner," he declared with a mock-leer. "Coffee?"

"Black, thank you."

He poured her a cup and handed it to her, smiling as she took a deep, healthy swallow and then gave a sigh of contentment. "Okay?" he asked.

"Wonderful," she nodded with the fervor of an inveterate, morning coffee-drinker. "With this kind of bedside manner, you must have a terrible problem with malingerers, Doctor."

"Oh, yes. Terrible," he chuckled.

She drank more coffee. "Is it late?" she wondered aloud.

"It depends on what you consider seven on a Sunday morning."

Her eyes widened. "Uncivilized."

"Ah—but you were in bed shortly after seven last night."

She slanted a look at him from beneath partially lowered lashes. "I may have been in bed," she informed him, "but I wasn't asleep. There *is* a difference."

"Oh, indeed there is," he agreed, his tone bringing a sudden rush of blood to her cheeks. "If it's too early for you, do you want to go back to bed—er—sleep?"

Mallory tossed her hair back over her naked shoulders. The bed linen slipped down several inches as she did so. "Once I'm up, I like to stay up," she replied, then glanced curiously at the napkin-covered wicker basket he'd included on the tray. Her stomach gave another little gurgle. "Is there something in there?" she asked hopefully. She couldn't remember when she'd been this hungry this early in the morning.

David flipped the napkin back. The delicious aroma of fresh-baked bread wafted out, teasing Mallory's nostrils. "Croissants," he announced, extending the basket to her with a small flourish.

"Mmm," she responded appreciatively, selecting one of the flaky, crescent-shaped rolls. She took a bite, chewed, and swallowed. "This is great!"

David nodded at a small glass bowl heaped full of what looked like strawberry or rasberry preserves. "Jam?"

"No, this is fine." In her opinion, the rich, buttery croissant needed no accompaniment.

He scooped a dollop of the glistening, deep-red jam with one finger. "It's homemade," he said temptingly.

"No, really," Mallory shook her head. The sheet slid down even further, revealing most of her creamy breasts.

"It's one of Mrs. Winslow's specialties."

"In that case, I'm sure it's delicious," Mallory said. She'd only met David's redoubtable housekeeper once, but she'd sampled quite a few examples of her culinary skill. "But I don't—"

A wicked gleam suddenly appeared in his eyes. "It goes with almost everything," he drawled. And, before she realized what he intended, he playfully daubed some of the jam onto the nipple of one of her bared breasts.

"Da—"

A split-second later, he bent his head and licked the rosy peak clean. The velvet stroke of his tongue on the sensitive tip triggered a lightning streak of excitement that arrowed straight into the core of her body.

"—vid!" Her voice went up. She just managed to put the coffee cup back down on the tray without spilling any of its contents on the bed...or David. She did, however, drop the uneaten portion of her croissant.

"A definite taste sensation," he declared and licked the rest of the jam off his finger. The teasing light in his eyes had become a distinctly sensual glint.

"You're crazy!" she tossed at him, tucking the sheets back up under her armpits. A small part of her brain mocked the move, telling her she was doing much too little, much too late, in the modesty department.

"If I am, it's your fault." He retrieved the roll she'd dropped after a brief search and put it back in the basket.

"Mine?"

"Uh-huh." He smiled at her slowly, with more than a hint of passion. "You're enough to drive a man right ...out...of...his...mind."

Between the last four words, he brought his mouth nearer hers an inch at a time. His voice softened as he spoke, muting to little more than a provocative whisper in the syllable before he entirely closed the distance between them and kissed her.

Their lips flirted and fused; their tongues darted and dueled. David cupped her face in his hands, his fingers threading through the softness of her dark curls. Mallory slid her palms up his sleekly muscled chest. His flesh was firm and warm and she thought she could feel his heart beating.

Gradually, the deep, hungry caress became a more playful exchange of kisses and gentle nips. Finally, Mallory eased back. Her brown eyes were glowingly seductive. Her lips looked lush and moist. David thought she was the most appealing woman he'd ever seen.

"Mmm . . . is that part of the Hitchcock bedside manner, too?" she asked throatily.

"Part of it, yes," he nodded. And, pressing her back against the pillows, he proceeded to demonstrate the rest.

They eventually got up and showered together. Any water they might have saved by taking one shower instead of two was more than offset by the length of time they lingered beneath the warm, gushing spray.

Once they dried each other off, they dressed and enjoyed a leisurely breakfast. After a call to the hospital drew the assurance that the emergency case of the day before was more than holding his own, they drove to Mallory's condominium so she could get a change of clothes.

"Is this yours?" David asked when she emerged from her bedroom. Clad in jeans, a faded blue cotton shirt, and a hazy navy and gray tweed jacket, he was standing by the piano, studying a partially completed sheet of handwritten music. He'd been picking out the notes quietly, trying to get a feel for the melody. He gave Mallory an interested, inquiring smile.

In the past, Mallory had always stubbornly refused to let people hear her compositions before they were polished to her satisfaction. It was an idiosyncrasy that had both amused and annoyed the other members of Fallen Angel, but they'd excused and accepted it on the grounds of creative temperament. Oddly enough, she didn't mind David's playing her unfinished song now. She felt a little shy about the situation, but her main concern was whether or not he would like it.

"It's just something I've been fooling around with," she told him. She'd put on a slim-fitting pair of jeans, her boots, and a man-tailored cream silk shirt worn like a tunic. She'd belted the top with an unusual woven strip of purple and blue cord. The buckle was a unique, free-form piece of hammered silver. She'd tamed her dark hair back into a tight knot at the nape of her neck and applied only a quick swipe of mascara and a light gloss of lip coloring for makeup.

"Is it a ballad?" David asked. There'd been a haunting lilt to the notes he'd been playing.

"It could be. I'm never quite sure how my songs are going to turn out." She made a ruefully funny face. "It's a little like having children, I guess. Do you—do you play?"

He spread his hands, holding them palms up. "I can read music to a point and hit the right keys about eighty per cent of the time, but I think it would be pushing things to say I actually play. My mother insisted I take lessons the year I turned ten. I think my teacher finally convinced her I was a lost cause."

"My dad taught me," Mallory said after a pause. "My mother played folk guitar. Before . . . before they died, we used to play together. It was—I liked it a lot." For a moment, her brown eyes were achingly full of memories.

"How old were you when your parents died?" David asked quietly, responding to the vulnerability he read in her face.

She plucked at the fringed ends of her belt for a second. "Twelve," she said flatly. "There was a car accident."

"What happened to you?"

"Afterward, you mean? I was put in foster homes. I didn't have any close relatives, and people don't usually like to adopt older kids. So I lived with a bunch of different families until I graduated from high school." She gave a little shrug. "That was a long time ago, though. It wasn't so bad."

It wasn't so good, either, David added silently, sensing the hurt she was doing her best to cover up. "Mallory—"

"What do you think of my song so far?" she asked,

changing the subject with no attempt at subtlety.

David glanced from her to the sheet music and back again. "I hope I can hear it when it's finished," he told her with unadorned sincerity.

"It may take quite awhile," she commented, feeling her heart skip a beat. "It's sometimes taken me weeks—even longer—to get a piece of music right."

"I don't mind waiting around." The expression in his blue-gray eyes was a promise.

Mallory wondered if she looked as pleased as she felt. "I'd like that," she answered and smiled.

They spent much of the rest of the day driving around. After Mallory had confessed that she had seen almost nothing of Farmington and the surrounding towns, David insisted on taking her on a guided tour of the area's most important sights. Some of the places were traditional tourist stops. Others were of a more personal nature, including the brick school building where David declared he had been kickball champion of the second grade and the snow-covered hill where he'd broken his collarbone and scarred his chin while trying to ski on his sled as an adventurous ten-year-old.

Impulse—and a lighthearted discussion of their childhood likes and dislikes—prompted a detour into Hartford for a stop at the famed Mark Twain House. The building, designed by Edward Tuckerman Potter and completed in 1874 at the then eyebrow-raising cost of $131,000, was an extravagant celebration of Victorian architecture. Mallory could have spent hours wandering around the whimsically furnished but palatial stone house where *Tom Sawyer, The Prince and the Pauper,* and other classics had been written. David shared her appreciation of the place and revealed that a youthful fondness for the works of Mark Twain had inspired him to spend an entire summer building a raft to float down the Farmington River. The raft, he told her, had sunk like a stone about six feet offshore.

They returned to David's house shortly after dusk with a sausage and mushroom pizza they'd picked up at a local take-out place. They ate it in the den in front of a roaring fire, washing down the impromptu meal with a bottle of Chianti.

"This is good pizza," Mallory remarked, licking a stray dribble of tomato sauce off her lower lip. She spoke with the conviction of a woman who had eaten pizza—to say nothing of every other kind of fast food known to man—from one end of the country to the other.

"Not bad," David agreed, scooping up another piece. "But the real test of pizza is how it tastes when it's reheated."

Mallory shook her head decisively, pulling a stretchy chunk of mozzarella cheese off the waxy paper that lined the cardboard pizza box and popping it in her mouth. "Nope," she contradicted.

"No?"

"The *real* test of pizza is how it tastes cold the morning after the night before."

"Ah." David nodded thoughtfully, draining the remaining red wine in his glass. He made a show of counting the pieces of pizza left in the box. "Well, we've got three and a half slices here. You can stick around and judge for yourself how they taste at breakfast tomorrow."

Mallory swirled her wine in her glass, keeping her expression demure. "That sounds . . . inviting." She slanted him a glance from beneath partially lowered dark lashes.

David smiled. Leaning forward, he relieved her of her glass. "And, in the meantime," he said, putting the glass down on the hearth, "let's try a little experiment about the benefits of reheating . . ."

A week and a half later, Mallory sat at the piano in her borrowed condominium, her brow furrowed with concentration. She repeated the musical phrase she had been toying with for the past ten minutes. The song was coming; she could feel it. Now all she had to do was let her ear take it the rest of the way. She went through the phrase again, her imagination supplying a subdued rhythm line and some subtle orchestration.

Subdued and subtle . . . something different. Not Molly V's usual style at all.

Closing her eyes, Mallory let the mood take her. Underneath the piano, her bare right foot tapped out a steady beat on the thickly carpeted floor as her slender fingers moved fluidly over the ivory and black keys.

She played a chord progression, humming along, searching for the heart of the still-changing melody. She knew this song was going to be something special . . . possibly even a love song.

A love song . . . for David?

Definitely something different.

The past ten days had been both special and different for her, thanks to David. In many ways, Mallory felt like a new woman; or perhaps she simply felt like the woman she was always intended to be. She had a man in her life who was both lover and friend—

The ringing of the phone interrupted this train of thought. David had had a meeting of an American Medical Association committee, but he'd promised to call and come over if it broke up early enough.

Anticipating this possibility, Mallory had moved one of the condo's several extension phones to within quick grabbing distance of the piano. She picked up the receiver now, her mouth forming a soft, expectant smile.

"Hello?" Her voice was low and warm.

"Molly, babe, how are you?"

Mallory's shoulders slumped. She suppressed a sigh of disappointment. "Oh, hi, Bernie."

"'Oh, hi, Bernie'?" her manager repeated. "I haven't talked to you in God knows how long and that's all I get?"

"Sorry," she apologized briefly. "I was expecting a call from someone else."

No, she was *hoping* for a call from someone else. If

she hadn't had her music to occupy her, she would have been hovering by the telephone like an overanxious teenager. She knew David well enough by now to be sure that he, unlike many other men of her acquaintance, would keep his promise to call her . . . *if* the AMA meeting got over at what he considered a decent hour.

Mallory didn't care if he called her at three in the morning. Chances were, she'd be awake. Despite some readjustments in her body's inner clock, she was still very much a creature of the night. It was one of the legacies of being on the road for ten years.

"Anybody I know?" Bernie asked, his suddenly sharpened tone cutting through her reflections.

"Anybody you know what?"

"This phone call you're expecting."

"Oh. No. You don't know him."

There was a pause on the other end. Mallory heard Bernie mutter a four-letter-word. "It's that guy, isn't it?" he asked heavily. "The one you were going out to dinner with the night you hung up on me. The one you wanted to look normal for." He swore again. "Dammit, I knew I shouldn't have let you talk me into letting you go off by yourself."

"What?" Her spine stiffened.

"You've been so sheltered—"

"Sheltered?" Isolated, maybe. Insulated, definitely. But sheltered? "If I'm so sheltered, Bernie, why are the details of my supposedly private life continually dished up for public consumption? For godsake, some tabloid is claiming I'm off having Bobby's baby!"

Bernie grunted. "You saw that piece of crap, huh?"

"Yes, I saw it," she snapped. "What are they going to write next? That I've had an abortion or a miscarriage? Or that I've given the baby up for adoption?"

"What's next is you and Colin Swann."

Mallory choked. She recalled Lori Hitchcock's curiosity about that particular subject. "Me and Swann?"

"Yeah. They doctored up a couple of old pictures. It looks—"

"Sleazy?" she suggested.

"Pretty hot, actually."

"Let me guess. Swann's comforting the grieving widow, right?"

"Right. Only you don't look too grieving. Hey, it's a natural angle, babe. Colin Swann steps in and saves the day by taking Bobby's place in the band—"

"So, naturally, everybody assumes he's taken Bobby's place in my bed, too," she finished.

"From what I hear, you could do a whole hell of a lot worse."

"Bernie!"

"Molly, when somebody like you drops out of sight the way you have, people are bound to wonder what's happening."

"Wondering is one thing. Making up lies is another."

"It goes with the territory. Besides, anybody who knows you—"

"What about people who *don't* know me?"

"Why should you give a damn—" Bernie broke off in midsentence. Mallory could practically hear his clever brain ticking over. "Don't ask me why, but I get the distinct feeling we're back to that guy again."

"He's not a guy," Mallory said, irritated beyond the point of discretion. "He's a doctor."

"A doctor? You got sick and you didn't tell me?"

"I haven't been sick. We—we met in a supermarket."

"What the hell were you doing in a supermarket?"

Mallory had to laugh at his appalled tone. "Shopping for groceries. David—we started talking. He asked me out to dinner and I said yes."

"How many times have you said 'yes' since then?"

Mallory stopped laughing. "Look, I don't want to—"

"Are you sleeping with him?" her manager asked bluntly.

"Bernie!"

"You *are* sleeping with him." Bernie sounded genuinely perturbed.

"I don't need your permission to—"

"Forget permission. I know you, Molly. Some of my clients can jump in and out of a different bed every night of the week. They think sex is nothing more than nature's way of saying hello. But you're not like that. I suppose you think you're in love with this David?"

Mallory clutched the telephone so hard her knuckles went a bloodless white. Love? Was that what she was feeling? A deep, powerful attraction, yes. But love? Certainly she knew there was a new tenderness in her, a new vibrancy that was finding its way into the song she was writing. But was she in love—?

Bernie apparently took her troubled silence as confirmation. "Let me guess," he went on. "You're thinking about honeymoons, right? Having *Good Housekeeping* fantasies?"

Mallory sucked in her breath, remembering how she'd felt being in David's home that first time. "What . . . what if I am?" she asked. "What . . . what would be wrong with that?"

"You'd be bored out of your gourd within six months and you know it."

"No, I *don't* know it," she retorted. "Look, has it ever occurred to you that I might like to do something different with my life?"

"Different? You've got the world by the tail!"

"I've got photographers popping out of my closets!"

"One photographer—*once*. And, hey, you've got to give the guy credit for tenacity. He waited in that closet for you for about forty-eight hours."

"What about the reporter who hid under the bed when Bobby and I were on our honeymoon?"

"The guy almost suffocated. Besides, you heard him wheezing before he had a chance to get any really juicy stuff down on tape."

"Bernie!" She didn't know whether to scream, laugh, or cry.

"You're a *star*, babe. It's what you wanted. It's what you've got. Okay, I appreciate that you're a little burned out. After what you've gone through in the last year or so, you're entitled. But you love who you are—what you do. I've seen you in front of an audience, Molly. God, you're like a lightning rod up there on stage. And when the applause hits, you're electric! You eat it up."

"Sometimes I feel like *it* eats me up," she said.

There was a silence.

"Have you told this guy who you are yet?" Bernie demanded finally.

Mallory bit her lip. Experience had taught her manager how to go for the jugular. When he needed to, he could wield words the way a surgeon wields a scalpel. "No," she admitted. "But I'm going to tell him."

"When?"

Soon, she promised herself. As soon as I can make sure how I feel about him . . . and he feels about me.

"You can't keep Molly V a secret forever, babe," Bernie warned. "Not even in Farmington, Connecticut."

"It's not going to be a secret forever. Just long enough."

"Long enough for what?"

"Long enough for David to really get to know Mallory Victor. Long enough so when I tell him about . . . about the rest . . . about Molly V . . . it won't make a difference."

Her manager gave a dubious snort. "It'll always make a difference," he declared. The flatly spoken words came out like a sentence that couldn't be appealed.

Two days later, those words came back to haunt her.

- 6 -

"NEON-BLUE EARRINGS AND AN electric-green sweat-shirt dress," David mused aloud wonderingly over a late lunch at the McDonald's at the West Farms shopping mall. He grinned across the table at Mallory. "Are you sure we aren't being too conservative?"

Mallory stole a french fry off his brown plastic tray and nibbled on it with a nicely calculated air of fashion superiority. "Electric-*blue* and neon-*green*," she corrected with precision.

"Thank you."

"You're welcome. Don't worry, David. Lori will love the birthday presents you picked out for her."

"*I* picked out? Mallory, I was thinking along the lines of a nice pair of designer jeans or some pastel T-shirts."

Mallory rolled her eyes in mock disdain as she calmly helped herself to another of his french fries. "You obviously don't understand contemporary fashion."

"Obviously. But if some of those outfits that girl was trying to sell us are examples of it, I think I'm better off *not* understanding."

"Coward," Mallory teased.

"Maybe," he laughed, glancing down at his tray. "Hey!" he exclaimed, swatting her hand lightly. "Eat your own french fries!"

Mallory managed to snitch three or four more of the golden-brown shoestrings. "I already have," she informed him saucily, popping several into her mouth. "I thought you said you like women who have healthy appetites and enjoy their food," she continued impishly, referring to his remarks during their first dinner together.

"Their food, not *mine,"* he clarified. "Do you want something else to eat?"

Mallory shook her head and dabbed daintily at her mouth with a napkin. "No, thank you," she refused with airy politeness. "I'm full."

"You're full of *my* french fries."

"Possessive aren't you?"

Blue-gray eyes met brown ones for a brief but heady moment. In that moment, the crowded and noisy restaurant they were sitting in vanished from Mallory's consciousness. A quiver of pleasure ran through her as David reached across the table, the humor suddenly gone from his strongly attractive face, and stroked his fingers down the back of her right hand.

"About some things, yes," he told her quietly. It was not an admission he made lightly. And it was not the kind of emotion any other woman had ever evoked in him.

"David—"

"Hey, Dr. David!" an enthusiastically shrill young voice interrupted. Two boys—both about seven or eight—suddenly appeared at David's elbow. One was towheaded, dressed in jeans and a hooded gray sweatshirt. The other was a freckled redhead with a ketchup smear on the corner of his mouth. He was wearing jeans, a Bruce Springsteen T-shirt, and a Yankees baseball jacket. He was the one who had spoken.

David turned. "Hi, Josh." He gave both boys a wide smile. "What are you doing here?"

"We're shoppin' with my dad. He's gettin' this anniversary present or somethin' for my mom. D'ya know how long they been married? *Ten years!*"

"That's quite a record," David observed.

"That's *forever,*" Josh's buddy piped up.

"Yeah," Josh agreed with a vigorous nod. He then apparently remembered his manners. "Uh—Dr. David, this is my friend, Bryan. Bry, this is my doctor. You know, I told you? He does magic tricks."

"Oh, yeah," Bryan acknowledged, giving David an interested look and a friendly smile. "Hi."

"Hi, Bryan," David returned. "And this is my friend, Mallory Victor. Mallory—Joshua and Bryan." He made the introductions without the slightest trace of adult-to-child condescension.

Mallory found herself being studied by two pairs of bright young eyes.

"Hi."

"Hi."

"Joshua . . . Bryan. Hello." She smiled.

"Is she your girl friend, Dr. David?" Josh asked curiously.

David glanced over at Mallory. She gazed back at him with limpid brown eyes and delicately raised brows. "Well, she's a girl—a woman—and she's a friend," he responded consideringly. "So I guess you can say she falls into that category."

Mallory contemplated kicking him under the table.

"I'm never gonna have a girl friend," Bryan announced firmly.

The vehemence in his voice amused Mallory, but she

was careful not to let it show. "Why not?" she asked.

The boy looked at her. "'Cause ya gotta do *mushy* stuff with them," he answered.

"Yeah, and most girls are dumb babies," Josh added. "Margaret Scott, this girl in my class, she had to get a shot 'cause she stepped on this rusty nail and they thought she might swell up and die or somethin'. Well, she *cried* just like some wimpy little kid."

"Shots can hurt," Mallory said, feeling she had to make some effort to defend her sex.

Dr. David gave me a shot once with a needle *this big*," Joshua said, indicating with his hands a needle about eighteen inches long. "And I didn't make a peep. I was only *six!*"

"You must be very brave," Mallory commented in what she hoped was a suitably respectful tone.

"Sure," Joshua confirmed with innocent arrogance. He glanced across the room. Following his eyes, Mallory saw a tall, chestnut-haired man signaling decisively. "Gotta go," the boy said. "Bye, Dr. David. Oh, hey, I shoulda thanked you for fixin' it so I could get my arm cast after they took it off. I got it hangin' on my wall and it looks *really* excellent."

"Glad to do it," David returned. "Just watch it with the tree climbing, though, buddy. All right?"

"Yeah, okay. Bye, lady. C'mon, Bry."

"Bye!"

The two youngsters darted off, narrowly missing colliding with a hefty middle-aged man carrying a tray heaped with hamburgers.

David and Mallory looked at each other and began laughing at the same time.

"Did you—did you really give him a shot with a needle *this big?*" Mallory asked, demonstrating the length of the needle with both hands as Joshua had done.

David reached across the table. Putting his palms against the backs of her hands, he gently pushed them together until they were about three inches apart. "It was barely this big," he told her with a smile. "And at the risk of violating doctor-patient confidentiality, the reason Josh didn't make a peep was that my nurse stuck a lollipop in his mouth right before I gave him the shot."

Their fingers intertwined intimately. "What about the magic tricks?"

"I do some simple sleight-of-hand for kids when they come in for their first appointment. It helps put them at ease."

"Even the dumb baby girls?"

One corner of his mouth curled. "I confess I save my best sleight-of-hand for smart, grown-up women."

"Mushy stuff, hmm?" His thumbs were massaging her wrists in slow, sensuous rotation.

David didn't need his excellent medical training to pick up the rapid throbbing of her pulse. "Definitely mushy," he agreed, stroking the silken skin of her inner arm. The taste and texture of that part of her—of every part of her—was indelibly burned into his memory.

"Do . . . all your patients call you 'Dr. David'?"

"Just the kids. Some of them have trouble saying Hitchcock, and rather than being referred to as Dr. Hiccup or Dr. Hidgecot, I settled for Dr. David."

"Dr. Hiccup?" Mallory's lips parted on a ripple of laughter.

He grinned at her. "The little charmer who thought that up has big brown eyes, too," he informed her. He released her hands before he was tempted to do more than just hold them.

She tilted her head, her unsteady fingers toying with the straw in her chocolate milkshake. "You seem to be very good with children," she observed. Unbidden, the thought occurred to her that for all his boyish—even childish—characteristics, Bobby hadn't been at ease with youngsters.

"I was a kid once, too," he remarked, shrugging off the compliment.

Mallory nibbled at her lower lip. "Have you . . . do you think about having children of your own?" she asked after a moment. He would make a wonderful father . . . and husband.

He didn't answer for a few seconds.

"Yes, I think about it," he replied at last, nodding slowly. "But I haven't done much beyond thinking. The time really hasn't been there. When I was younger, I was caught up in becoming a doctor . . . and now—"

He paused, drumming his strong, lean fingers on the plastic tabletop. His eyes were oddly reflective.

And now, he was caught up in being a doctor. But he did think about having a family. He was thinking about it. And the thoughts he was having included a miniature Mallory: a dark-haired, dark-eyed little girl dressed in bright, rainbow colors.

For a moment, he was tempted to tell her just how deep his feelings for her were. But his uncertainty about her reaction held him back. Physically, he and Mallory had no secrets from each other. She'd given him her body—open and offering—without constraint. But her mind and her heart remained frustrating mysteries to him in many ways. There were times when Mallory seemed the most elusive woman he had ever met; trying to learn her secrets was like trying to nail down quicksilver.

"Do you ever think about having a family?" he asked her finally.

"Oh, yes," she replied. Her voice was soft but sincere. For a moment, her brain filled with the image of a baby boy with wide, blue-gray eyes; a dandelion-puff of sandy-brown hair; and a crook-cornered little smile. For a moment, the image was so real, she could almost feel the child in her arms . . . at her breast—

"Did you and your husband—?" David questioned. He didn't understand the source of the half-dreamy, half-sad expression on her face, but it tore at him.

Mallory looked at him. Couldn't he see? For all that she was still holding back from him, she felt as transparent as glass around him sometimes. She wondered what he would do if she told him the family she'd been thinking of was his—theirs.

"Bobby and I . . . we never really settled down enough for a family. With our careers we had to travel so much. The time just never seemed right."

There was a pause.

"The time just never seems right for a lot of things," David observed enigmatically. He took a few seconds and glanced around the restaurant. "So," he said, his eyes coming back to Mallory, "shall we finish shopping for Lori?"

"Good idea," she agreed. She didn't know whether she was relieved or regretful at his decision to close the subject of having families.

After clearing their table, they went back out into the mall. The place was even more crowded than it had been before they'd stopped for lunch. People were thronging in either to take advantage of final, end-of-winter clearance sales or to check out the latest spring-summer merchandise. David slipped a companionable arm around Mallory's waist as they walked along, his hand resting casually against her hip.

Mallory had had some anxieties about this shopping trip. The thought of going out among so many people had made her feel uncomfortably vulnerable. That sense of vulnerability had faded, however, as she and David made their way in leisurely fashion around West Farms. Oh, she'd been eyed a few times, but she was experienced enough to know the difference between a foxy-lady stare of assessment and an I-know-you! double take.

"Actually," David commented as he maneuvered her around a pretty young woman pushing a stroller, "I don't know why I'm concerned about the presents I'm giving

Lori this year. If I tell her you picked them out, she'll love them."

"Why do you say that?"

He smiled. "She's your biggest fan."

His choice of words brought her up short. Mallory experienced a flash of panic. Good God, had Lori said something?

"I—what do you mean?" she got out in a reasonably calm voice, hoping she hadn't gone as white as she felt.

David sensed—but didn't understand—her sudden tension. "I just meant that you made quite an impression on her the day you met at my house. That must have been some salad you fixed her."

Mallory relaxed slightly. "Why do you say that?"

"Because each time I've spoken to her during the past week and a half, she's told me to say 'hi' and 'thanks for the salad.'" He chuckled. "I've never heard anyone put so much significance into the word *salad*, either."

Mallory shrugged. "What can I say?" she asked lightly, "I make a terrific salad."

"Modesty is such a becoming quality," he told her.

"Funny, that's not what you said last night in the bathtub."

"Well, *im*modesty has its points, too," he quipped.

"And of course—" Mallory stopped suddenly, realizing where he was heading. "Oh, you're not getting Lori a record, are you?" she asked, her body tightening again.

David halted, too. "Is there something wrong with that?"

Trying not to panic at the idea, Mallory searched for a suitable way of diverting him from his destination. "It—I—it's just not a very original thought," she said lamely.

Her obvious nervousness puzzled him. "Lori said she wanted an album for her birthday," he said reasonably. "And this is one area where I really need your help, Mallory. I don't have a clue as to *which* album she wants. Frankly, in my opinion, most of the alleged music my sister listens to has only one distinguishing characteristic: It's loud. If you don't give me some advice, I'll probably wind up giving her Lawrence Welk." He took her arm. "Original or not, it's what she wants."

"But I can't—"

"You can." Forcefully he steered her into the record store. Mallory was helpless to protest. Panicked, she gazed around her. With its poster-covered walls, merchandise-crammed racks, chattering clientele, and blaring sound system, this particular record store seemed identical to every other record store she had ever been in—and she had been in quite a few. She winced inwardly as her wary gaze focused briefly on a life-size cardboard cutout of an internationally known rock singer who had once made a drunken pass at her. She'd ended up kneeing him in the groin when it had become frighteningly clear that he wasn't going to take no for an answer.

"Here we are," David said. "Rock, rock, and more rock."

"Here we are," Mallory echoed faintly. She allowed herself to be pulled toward the bins where the rock records were stored.

Afterward, she asked herself if things might have gone differently if they'd begun at the end of the alphabet instead of the beginning.

She was flipping methodically through the *C* albums when she felt the eyes. Stomach tightening, she looked up. She swiftly realized that the source of her instinctive uneasiness was a knot of five or six teenagers standing about ten feet away. They were staring at her, whispering excitedly and pointing. One of the teenagers—a shaggy-haired, jeans-clad boy—was clutching an open copy of *Rolling Stone* magazine and nodding vigorously.

Oh, no, she thought desperately, dropping her eyes. Her heart was pounding. Her worst fears were being realized—or almost her worst fears.

David was now standing at the record bin next to her, going through the albums there with a mixture of interest and appalled amusement. Where in heaven's name do they find these people? he wondered. And who comes up with—

At that moment he froze. Sitting at the front of the collection of *F* albums was a number of recordings by a group called Fallen Angel. The name rang a faint bell. The picture on the front of an album entitled "Tumble to Earth" did more than that.

The cover was a smoky-toned, full-length portrait of a woman who seemed to be part enchantress, part street-wise urchin. From the waist up, she was dressed in a diaphanous white lace blouse and ropes of pearls and crystal beads. Her dark hair was blown into sensual disorder by some mysterious breeze. From the waist down, she wore a black leather miniskirt, sheer black stockings, and high-heeled black shoes. A pair of white-feathered wings lay at her feet.

The woman in the portrait was Mallory Victor. But the name on the record jacket read Molly V.

"David—" Trying to keep track of the group of staring teenagers without actually meeting their eyes—a serious mistake in this kind of situation, she knew—Mallory put a hand on David's arm. She calculated the distance to the exit.

"This is you, isn't it, Mallory?" David asked in a taut voice, still holding the album. Lord, he knew that exquisitely expressive face, that slenderly feminine body. And he'd thought he knew—or at least was beginning to know—the woman they belonged to as well. But now—*now* what was he supposed to think?

David's tone brought her up short, driving her concern about being recognized by the teenagers right out of her mind. She looked at him apprehensively, searching for words. David was staring at her as though he were seeing her for the first time . . . and not quite liking what he saw.

"This is you, isn't it, Mallory," he repeated. It wasn't a question this time. He had the primitive desire to shake an answer out of her. Of all the things he'd speculated about in trying to fill in the holes in her background, this certainly had not been one of them.

"David—" She big her lip painfully, damning the betraying album cover. Of all the ways she'd envisioned David learning the truth about her, this certainly had not been one of them!

"Or should I say *Molly?*" There was a slashing emphasis on the last word.

He shouldn't have said Molly. He *certainly* shouldn't have said it loudly enough to put to rest whatever lingering doubts had been holding the gawking teenagers back from approaching her.

Things happened with an almost frightening rapidity after that. In what seemed like a matter of seconds, Mallory was surrounded by a throng of fans. They were eager, enthusiastic, and encroaching, trapping her against the record bin as they called out questions, asked for autographs, and reached forward to touch her.

Ten years in rock-and-roll had taught Mallory some painful lessons about the volatile chemistry of crowds, although it had been a long time since she'd had to contend with this many people, this close, without the buffer of a manager, a bodyguard, or a full-scale entourage. This crowd of fans seemed friendly enough now, but she knew that could change in a flash if she didn't give them what they wanted.

"Molly, Molly—over here!"

"It's *her*—"

"I touched her. *I touched her!*"

"Sign this! Sign this!"

"—Colin Swann?"

"Sing!"

What they wanted was Molly V.

Still off balance from the shock of his discovery, David

found himself shoved aside in the first moments of madness. But, even in the confusion, he never lost sight of Mallory. Seeing her initial, panicky reaction, he began elbowing his way into the crowd.

"Let the lady have some room, please," he said in a sharp voice as he reached Mallory. Remarkably, the crowd responded to his tone of authority. The people closest to Mallory edged back slightly, leaving her feeling simply crowded, not claustrophobic.

David slipped a half-possessive, half-protective arm around her waist. "Are you okay?" he asked in an undertone. His immediate concern was her safety. David didn't have any personal experience with this sort of situation, but he'd studied enough psychology to know that it had to be handled carefully.

Mallory nodded once, giving him a sidelong, desperately grateful look. A part of her—the part that had learned not to trust or to expect too much from other people—had feared that he might simply walk away or stand aside. That he was sticking with her gave her a rush of confidence.

"Who's he?" somebody demanded.

"A friend," Mallory returned instantly. Without really thinking about what she was doing, she shifted her posture slightly, tossed her hair back, and summoned up her sharpest, sexiest smile. They wanted Molly V—they'd get her. It was the only way she knew how to deal with what was happening. She tried not to think about how she was going to deal with what was going to happen afterward.

David felt the transformation more than saw it. Awareness of the change rippled through him. It was a subtle but palpable thing. In the space of a few seconds, Mallory Victor altered the way she held herself, tilted her head, pitched her voice. She became a different woman . . . a stranger.

A rock star named Molly V.

At this point, the record store's assistant manager stepped in. A young man with an entrepreneur's instinct for taking advantage of any and all opportunities, he waded into the still-growing crowd and loudly announced that she would be happy to sign autographs for everyone if people would just let her move to the counter at the front of the store. He then latched onto Mallory like a human leech. Ten seconds later, Side One of "Tumble to Earth" started blasting through the sound system.

David let her go. He had no other choice.

Mallory got through the next half hour on automatic pilot. She signed, she smiled, she shook her head to the too-personal questions and the requests for a song. It was an expert, experienced performance that would have pleased Bernie McGillis if he'd seen it. It might even have convinced Mallory herself if she hadn't felt the need to seek out David with her eyes every few minutes. It was as though she were a compass needle and he were the magnetic North Pole: He gave her a sense of being able to keep her bearings.

The tenth or eleventh time she glanced over toward the spot where he had taken position—watching, waiting—he was no longer there. Shaken, she looked around. She couldn't find him.

She felt as though she'd been dynamited from the inside out.

Like a rock-and-roll robot, she signed autographs for another ten minutes or so. Still no David.

He *was* gone.

Then a pair of uniformed security guards marched into the record store with the air of being men on a mission. They were a mismatched couple: one tall and cadaverously thin, the other short and bulky.

"Ma'am?" the shorter guard addressed her politely.

Startled, Mallory looked up from the record cover she

was signing. Now what? she asked herself.

"Your car is waiting," the same guard said. His partner nodded.

"Car—?" Her rented car was parked back at her borrowed condominium.

"Dr. Hitch—"

"Oh!" In an instant, she was Mallory Victor again.

Despite the very vocal protests of the remaining crowd, the guards extricated her from the record shop and hustled her through the mall with more speed than ceremony. They were so briskly businesslike that Mallory felt more like a suspected shoplifter than a celebrity.

David was waiting for her in his car. It was parked next to the curb with the motor running. As she came out into the sunlight, he leaned across the front seat and opened the door on the passenger's side. After a few words of thanks to the guards, she got in and shut the door.

"Thank you," she said as he shifted gears and pulled away. Settling into the seat, she sighed. Unconsciously, she rubbed at the tattoo on her inner right wrist, almost as though she were trying to erase it.

"For what?" David asked, catching the movement out of the corner of his eye. His inflection was stony and his profile set.

"Getting me out of that mess."

"You *did* want to be gotten out, then?"

She looked at him. "Yes, of course! Do you think I enjoyed that?"

Inside his head, his memory was replaying her transformation. "I'm not sure what to think," he returned. They were at the exit of the parking lot. The light up ahead turned green. David hit the horn as the car in front of them remained motionless. "You're a true performer . . . Mallory."

The compliment—if it was that—was double-edged.

The pause before her name was equally cutting. "David, I was going to tell—"

"I bought your latest album. You'll have to autograph it for Lori."

Her stomach started to churn. "She already has it," she said unwisely.

David took his eyes off the road for a moment, pinning her to her seat.

"Remember the album she kept playing this summer when she stayed with you? The one you told her was driving you nuts?" It was stupid to goad him, she knew, but she couldn't help herself. "That was—is—my latest album."

"Lori knows who you are." The quicksilver flashes in his eyes turned to ice. He knew it was stupid to feel so angry, but he couldn't help himself.

"David—" Somehow, she had to explain.

"Leave it until we get to your place," he bit out.

They made the rest of the drive in silence.

"Why didn't you tell me, Mallory. Or is it really *Molly?*"

She had taken up refuge in the corner of the modular sofa arrangement in the living room of the condominium. He was standing about five feet away.

"Mallory Victor is my real name. I'm known professionally as Molly V."

"Of Fallen Angel." He started to pace. Mentally, he tried to reconcile the woman on the sofa with the woman he'd seen signing autographs in the record store . . . with the woman he'd seen on the album cover. It wasn't easy.

Mallory nodded mutely, following him with wary eyes.

"Like your tattoo."

Is it supposed to be you? he'd asked her that first night.

"Like my tattoo," she confirmed quietly.

I've been accused of being a lot of things, she'd told him over dinner. But an angel isn't one of them.

"Why didn't you tell me?" he repeated.

She closed her eyes, listening to the pounding of her heart.

"Mallory?"

At least he hadn't said Molly again.

She opened her eyes and looked up at him. "I didn't tell you because I was afraid."

David stopped pacing, feeling as though he'd been slapped across the face. "You were afraid?" he echoed in disbelief. "You were afraid of *me?*"

"Of how you'd react if—when—you found out."

Her words stunned him. "What did you think I was going to do? Act like those kids in the record store?"

"Of course not!" she denied. Oh, Lord, how was she going to explain? As her feelings for him had grown over the past days, she'd come closer and closer to having the confidence in their relationship to tell him the truth. But now . . .

"Then *what?*" he demanded. "Look, I can accept your not wanting to say anything at the beginning. I mean, 'oh, by the way, I'm a rock star' isn't exactly something you can just casually toss into a conversation with someone you've barely met. But later! After we got to know each other . . . after we made love—"

After you became such an important part of my life, he added silently. You . . . whoever you are.

"You told Lori!" he accused.

Mallory bit the inside of her lip hard. The coppery taste of blood tainted her mouth. She sensed a change in the quality of David's anger, but she couldn't understand it. "I didn't tell her. She recognized me."

"But you asked her not to tell me."

She looked away. "Yes," she admitted, feeling miserable. She'd been wrong to do that. Her reasons had seemed right at the time, but she'd been wrong—terribly wrong.

David gave a sardonic laugh. "Well, I have to give you credit. I don't think Lori's ever kept a secret before."

Mallory searched for the words to repair the damage. "It's not—I . . . I wanted to tell you myself."

"When?"

"I don't know. But I *was* going to tell you."

"Were you?" he pressed.

"*Yes!*" Her brown eyes held a profound sadness. After a long, wrenching moment, she buried her face in her palms. "You don't understand," she said.

Closing the physical distance between them in three swift strides, David sat down beside her. He pulled her hands away from her face, his fingers locking around her wrists as if he didn't ever intend to let go. The expression on his craggily featured face was fierce.

"Then help me to understand, Mallory," he urged intensely. He tightened his grip. "I want to understand. Dammit, I *need* to understand. Don't be afraid of me . . . please."

"David—"

"Please. *Trust me.*"

Where Mallory Victor was concerned, she did trust him—completely. But when it come to Molly V . . .

"Please," he repeated.

She hesitated, struggling to put the words, the emotions, the experiences, in order. "It's so hard," she said slowly. She was acutely conscious of his touch. His lean-fingered doctor's hands were very strong and yet . . . he wasn't hurting her.

He wouldn't hurt her.

She looked at him. "You know, in some ways, I think you understand me better than anyone else," she said. "But in others . . . how could you? We're from two different worlds."

"The doctor and the rock star?" His tone had softened slightly.

"Something like that," she nodded. "I—after my parents were killed, I felt totally alone. It didn't seem as if anybody wanted me or loved me. I didn't have *anything* ... except music. That was mine. I was good at it, even back then."

David heard both pride and pain in her voice. "So?" he prompted.

"So ... I decided to use it. I decided to become a star—somebody everybody would want and love." Her eyes clouded. "God, it all seemed so simple."

"A lot of things seem simple when you're young," David observed quietly. There was more to his tone than agreement. He was thinking about himself at fourteen.

Mallory nodded. "Yes, they do," she said, then took a deep breath. "I met Bobby Donovan when I was nineteen. He and I—that seemed simple, too." She worried the inner right corner of her lip for a moment. "He was the lead guitarist for a group called Fallen Angel. They weren't exactly a chartbusting success back then, but I didn't care. I joined Bobby and the rest of them on the road. At first, it wasn't easy. I mean, as far as the other guys were concerned, I wasn't anything more than Bobby's old lady and another mouth to feed. But we got close fairly quickly." She smiled at the memory. "You tend to do that when you're crammed together in a van or sleeping five to a cheap motel room. Anyway, after a while, I started singing with them ... and writing some songs."

"A star was born?"

"Molly V was born. Or at least named. We all used to introduce ourselves near the end of our gigs. One night at a dive in New Jersey, a man in the audience misheard my first name. He thought I said Molly V. He was drunk, I guess, because he started chanting Molly V. Then everybody was chanting it. Don't ask me why. It was amazing. It made me feel . . . special. I was standing there on this grungy little stage and all these people were calling for *me*." She laughed. "Anyway, the name stuck. I liked it. The band liked it. And Bernie McGillis liked it, too."

"Bernie McGillis?"

"My manager. He found Fallen Angel—me—about eight years ago and signed us up. Four months later, I turned on a radio and heard myself singing a song I'd written. A year after that, Fallen Angel won two Grammy Awards and Bobby decided we should get married."

"You had everything you'd wanted." Without quite understanding why, David thought of the old admonition: Be careful what you wish for; you just might get it.

"Everything I'd wanted," she repeated.

"What happened?" he asked after a moment. It was obvious from her expression that something had.

She twisted a lock of hair around one finger in a gesture he had become achingly familiar with. "I stopped being so young and things stopped being so simple."

"Your . . . husband?" It was the only possibility he could think of. Judging from the reaction in the record store, there was nothing wrong with her career. "Did your success—?"

"Oh, no. He was Molly V's biggest fan in some ways. Besides, he was successful, too. And no matter how old Bobby got, everything stayed simple for him. He'd get out in front of an audience, night after night, like a starving child let loose in a candy store, and he'd lose himself in the applause, the adulation. I . . . I guess I did the same thing, in the beginning. But Bobby never got tired of it. The only things he ever got tired of were his toys, and he had enough money to buy plenty of new ones."

"Toys?"

"Fast cars, fast boats . . . fast women." Suddenly afraid

of the emotions she was dredging up, she averted her eyes. "There . . . he was with somebody else when he crashed his boat. She died, too."

Finally releasing her wrists, David leaned forward and hooked two fingers under her chin. He gently forced her to face him. He clamped down on the desire to tell her that her late husband sounded like a selfish, immature bastard who didn't deserve the grief he thought he read in her expression.

"Mallory, I'm sorry," he said. "But all this—I still don't understand why you were afraid to tell me about Molly V."

"I thought you'd be . . . horrified."

"Why? Because I said your music drove me nuts?" He shook his head and bit back a smile, fleetingly damning his half sister's in-the-ears-out-the-mouth tendencies. "Mallory, Lori had the stereo turned up to the threshold of pain last summer. She could have been playing Mozart—"

Mallory shook her head. "David, you're the type of man who gets in the newspaper for receiving a Presidential citation. As Molly V . . . I get my face smeared across the tabloids. I've got an image. Because I'm pretty uninhibited on stage . . . you see, I perform—"

"As you did in the record store?" He thought he was beginning to understand.

"*Yes!*" she nodded eagerly. "I'm not really like that. Not deep down. Oh, I admit I've done some things— gone along with some ideas of Bernie's—that wouldn't exactly qualify me for membership in the Junior League, but—" She spread her hands, watching him hopefully. "In the beginning, I wanted the publicity. The attention. I didn't mind the gossip. It was a case of not really caring what people wrote about me as long as they *did* write about me. For a while, it was almost like reading about somebody else. I mean, I'd see 'Molly V is doing this' and 'Molly V is doing that' and it didn't seem real because I wasn't doing any of those things. But then . . . they started writing about my—about me and Bobby."

David swore, low and lethal.

Mallory licked her suddenly dry lips. "I knew Bobby had other women. He never hid them. In a way, I think that helped me to tell myself that they weren't really important to him."

"But how—why did you put up with it?"

"I did love him . . . in a way," she said slowly. "In the beginning, when we were both so young . . . so ambitious. And Fallen Angel was like another family. I belonged to them and they belonged to me. I'd already lost one family, David . . . I was afraid—I put up with Bobby's infidelities because I was afraid of losing another."

Dropping her eyes, Mallory drew a deep steadying breath. David wanted to reach out and take her in his arms, but he held back, sensing she had more to say.

"I am Molly V, yes," she went on. "But that's only part of who I am. Most people can't—or won't—get beyond that. It seems the wrong people are turned on and the right ones are turned off without ever realizing that there's more to me than—than—oh, what they see on a stage or a record cover. They react to the image— the mask—not to me. And that's why I didn't tell you, David. I–I didn't want Molly V to get in the way. I wanted you to know Mallory Victor first."

There was a long silence. Finally, Mallory looked up; Bernie's cynical assertion that Molly V would always make a difference echoed forebodingly through her brain.

The expression in David's blue-gray eyes silenced that echo quickly. His eyes held understanding and warmth.

"David?" she whispered wonderingly. He was looking at her—*her!*—with such tenderness . . .

"You and I want the same thing," he told her simply. "I do know Mallory Victor . . . now."

There was nothing more to say—at least not then. And there was no reason for him to hold back from taking her in his arms and showing her how well he knew her ... and how much he cherished what he knew.

- 7 -

"YOU KNOW, YOU NEVER did answer Lori's question this evening," David remarked thoughtfully four nights later. He was sitting on the edge of the king-size bed in the master bedroom of Mallory's borrowed condominium, watching her undress with a sense of possessive pleasure. He'd already stripped down to a pair of white cotton briefs that felt as if they were getting briefer with each article of clothing Mallory removed.

"What question was that?" Mallory asked, stretching languidly, then picking up her hairbrush. She was clad only in a black, lace-trimmed camisole and matching bikini panties.

She was not unaware of the effect she was having on David; in fact, she was enjoying it. No, positively reveling in it. She was playing the temptress with a relish she had never experienced before. Telling David the truth—and having him accept it—had liberated her somehow. She felt free to be herself.

"The one about how long you're planning to stay in Farmington." He'd approached the subject obliquely several times during the past four days, but she'd always evaded it.

Keep pushing, Hitchcock, a voice inside his head warned, and you may get an answer you don't want to hear.

But what answer *did* he want to hear? Throughout his adult life, David Hitchcock had always subordinated his personal life to his professional one. However, his feelings for Mallory were reaching the point where he didn't think he'd be able to subordinate them to anything— including his work.

Yet he'd promised himself a long time ago, his work would be put *first,* no matter the cost.

Only a hint of these thoughts appeared on his face, but it was enough to send a tremor of anxiety darting through Mallory. She hid her uncertainty behind a toss of her head and a deceptively light laugh.

"Tired of me already, Dr. Hitchcock?"

Brown eyes met blue-gray.

"No way," he said, smiling with a flippancy he wasn't feeling. "The rock world's loss is definitely my gain."

He wondered what she would do if he told her how deeply he had come to care for her. Would she think such a confession was somehow linked to her disclosures about Molly V? Although he didn't fully understand it, he realized that Mallory was very ambivalent about her professional persona—particularly when it came to men's responses to it. He hadn't told her how he felt about her before he knew she was Molly V; if he told her just four days after finding out...

Mallory smiled at him. "I'm glad you appreciate what you've got," she said, wishing he hadn't answered her question so glibly.

"Appreciate?" He leaned back a bit, supporting himself on his forearms. "After all the things Lori said about Molly V tonight, I'm in awe."

"Don't be," Mallory said, giving her hair several more strokes with the brush. Her dark curls crackled around her head and shoulders in an electrically charged cloud. "Some of those stories were more than a little exaggerated."

"Too bad," he chuckled, his eyes going over her with gleaming male assessment. "Some of those stories were more than a little intriguing."

A frisson of excitement danced up Mallory's spine. David could increase her awareness of her femininity tenfold without even touching her. And when he *did* touch her...

"I think things went well tonight, don't you?" she asked.

"I'm hoping they'll go even better now that Lori's gone."

"David!" she laughed. "I'm serious."

Partly because she'd wanted to assure herself that she hadn't caused any lasting trouble between Lori and David—and partly because she genuinely liked the teenager—Mallory had asked David to invite his half sister to the condominium for supper. Aside from the This is Your Life, Molly V flavor of Lori's exuberant dinner table talk, Mallory thought things had worked out very well. But she wanted to be certain.

"I think Lori had a terrific time," he told her honestly. "You didn't mind posing for those Polaroids? Or signing thirty-seven copies of *The Hartford Courant*?"

"No, I didn't mind. But it was thirty-*nine* copies."

"I suppose you big rock stars notice things like that."

"Very funny." She brandished the brush at him for a moment. "I suppose your ego was bruised because she didn't ask for your autograph, too." An account of what had happened at the West Farms Mall had appeared in

The Hartford Courant three days before. Headlined "Rock Star Causes Near Riot," it had been relatively straight-forward, and full of quotes from the store's enterprising assistant manager. Lori had lugged a huge stack of the newspapers to the condo with her, and wheedled Mallory into signing each one in the margin next to the article.

"Why should she have asked me? My name wasn't mentioned."

"Well, thank heaven for that," Mallory murmured fervently. So far, the only fallout from the near-fiasco at West Farms had been an angry phone call from a very irate Bernie McGillis. He'd demanded to know what she thought she was doing, making unscheduled personal appearances. Her explanation of what had happened had barely mollified him.

"Thank heaven?" Both David's brows went up.

"Mmm . . ." Putting down her brush, she crossed over to him, fitting herself intimately between his firmly muscled thighs. She supposed it was inevitable that word of her relationship with David was going to get out, but she was praying it would happen later rather than sooner. She trailed her fingertips delicately over his naked shoulders. "You can't imagine what it would be like if people found out we're—ah . . ."

"Involved?" He stroked the backs of her legs. "But we are." And getting more involved all the time, he thought.

"If people found out, you'd have reporters crawling all over you."

He paid teasing, tactile homage to the silken skin of her inner thighs. "I confess, I'd rather have *you* crawling all over me."

"David!" She pulled back slightly. Well, given his stable self-assurance and integrity, maybe David Hitchcock was one of those rare men who could go through the media meat grinder and come out whole, but she didn't think he'd like the experience . . . or the person who brought it on him.

"Mallory—" He pulled her close again.

"This isn't funny," she said. "What would you do if a reporter showed up on your doorstep and asked if you were having an affair with me?"

David hesitated. "Actually, a reporter did call me yesterday," he told her after a few seconds.

"What?" She stared at him, feeling herself going pale.

"I didn't mention it because it didn't seem that important," he explained. He also hadn't mentioned it because he hadn't wanted to upset her over what he considered nothing more than a minor annoyance.

"Didn't seem—"

"Mallory—" His hands moved over her soothingly. "It's all right. One phone call from one reporter. I managed. He asked me if I knew Molly V and I told him no." He smiled.

"You . . . lied." She relaxed slightly. One phone call from one reporter. Maybe . . . maybe . . . they'd be lucky— this time.

"Yes."

But had he? he wondered. In all honesty, David didn't feel he knew Molly V. Oh, he'd listened to the Fallen Angel album he'd bought—and been unexpectedly impressed. He'd even spent a lunch hour at the local library going through back copies of *Rolling Stone,* reading about Mallory's career—and been impressed again. But that didn't mean he knew Molly V.

"Only one phone call from one reporter?" she reiterated.

"Yes," he repeated firmly. He was relieved when he felt her relax. "It's nothing to be concerned about. I just wonder how the guy got my name in the first place."

"There are lots of ways, believe me," she said dryly. If he'd used a credit card to buy her album, that could be traced. If someone had seen the license of the car she'd gotten into at the Mall, that could be traced, too. Oh, yes, there were lots of ways. "But if another reporter calls—"

"I'll tell him it's none of his damned business." Gathering her very close, he pressed his mouth against the perfumed, shadowed cleft between her breasts.

"That won't—ah—work."

"Okay, I'll say we're good friends." His lips were searing through the sheer fabric of her camisole.

"O—only people who are m—more than good friends say that." What he was doing to her was a lot more good than it was friendly.

"I'll have to lie again, then." Slipping his hands up under the camisole, he began tracing erotic designs on her back.

"David—"

"No comment."

"Mmm—what?"

"I'll say no comment," he elaborated a bit raggedly, his hands drifting downward. He slipped two fingers underneath the waistband of her bikini underpants.

"W—wonderful idea." She wasn't thinking about the press anymore.

Neither was he. "Mallory, good Lord, you're driving me crazy!"

"Blood rushing to your brain, hmm?" Dipping her head, she kissed the side of his neck.

"It's—ah-ha—certainly rushing *somewhere* . . ."

She kissed the other side of his neck. His pulse beat strongly against her lips. "Do you want to discuss your symptoms?"

He chuckled. "I should think one of them is fairly obvious by now."

"Fairly," she agreed, a delicious sense of languor invading her body. The hardened male length of him pressed against her. "Do you . . . think it's . . . serious?" She linked her arms around his neck.

"It could be without proper—ah—attention."

"What about *im*proper attention?" Tiny arrows of flame darted along her nervous system.

"Even better," he assured her. Desire throbbed through every inch of his body, desire it would take a few ecstatic minutes to assuage but a lifetime to satisfy. He began undoing the tiny satin ribbons that held the front of her camisole closed. Fortunately for his none-too-steady fingers, the knots gave way easily. Cupping her bared breasts in his hands, he circled the pink crests with his thumbs, watching as the responsive buds came to attention under his ministrations.

Mallory's head tilted back and she closed her eyes. "Mmm . . . that feels so good," she breathed.

"I told you the first time we made love I wanted to know everything you like," he reminded her huskily, relishing the play of emotions across her face.

"You know things I didn't realize I li—hi—iked!" Lord, was it because he was a doctor that he knew her body's secrets so completely? That he knew exactly where and when and how to touch? Her knees turned to jelly and she melted against him.

David pulled her down on top of him, welcoming her slender weight and seductive warmth. Their mouths fused in a heated, hungry kiss, their tongues mating and meshing in a passionate joust.

The briefs went, followed almost immediately by the camisole and bikini panties. Mallory nibbled a dainty path down the cord of his neck and licked along the strongly defined lines of his collarbone, sampling the smooth texture and faintly salty taste of his skin. She quested through the sandy-brown mat of his chest hair, seeking the tightly furled tips of his nipples. Those treasures discovered and claimed, she kissed her way downward, her hair drifting over his body. She was wanton in the generosity of her appreciation of him.

"Mallory, sweetheart—" His hands marauded over her quivering, receptive form, inciting riots of pleasure as they moved. Like a virtuoso, he played her until every fiber of her being was singing its need for him. Each sigh . . . each sob . . . each shudder . . . was like music.

Finally, strong and sure, he surged up over her, taking all she offered, giving all she demanded. Mallory came up to meet him, arching in ancient invitation and wrapping her arms and legs around him.

There was a moment of mutual selfishness followed by a moment of mutual surrender. After that, what they shared was no longer a matter of moments.

Two reporters called David at his office the next day. They were better informed and more insistent than the first journalist, but David gave them both a flat no comment.

He didn't mention the calls to Mallory when he saw her that night.

The same two reporters and three new ones called up the day after that. When one of them became especially rude, David hung up. When he left for the day, he shrugged off the sharply curious look he got from his receptionist with a muttered, "We're just good friends."

He did mention what was going on to Mallory that night, but he made light of the situation, making the calls sound more amusing than irritating.

The next day, a stringer from UPI appeared on his doorstep along with a free-lance photographer. David played deaf when a reporter fired off a list of highly personal questions. He was nearly blinded when the photographer popped a flashbulb in his face.

After his vision cleared, he trenchantly informed the pair that they were on private property. He then proceeded to persuade them that he was definitely serious about having them both hauled off for trespassing.

He took a long and circuitous route when he drove to see Mallory that night. Part of him felt like a paranoid fool for doing so. The rest of him was relieved that no one followed him.

They spent the weekend at the condominium. There were no reporters . . . no ringing telephones.

It was just the two of them. And it seemed perfect.

There were reporters and photographers waiting for him when he reached his office on Monday morning, all of them clamoring to know the details of his weekend rendezvous with Molly V. Several of them countered his teeth-gritted no comment by waving a reprint of a wire service photograph under his nose. He was stunned when he realized it was a copy of one of the pictures Lori had taken of him and Mallory when she'd come to the condominium for dinner.

"Where did you get this?" he demanded. Lord, had they been after Lori, too?

"We've got sources, Doc—where's Molly V?"

"How does it feel to be Molly V's latest?"

"How did you meet her, Doc?"

David lost his temper. "In the fruit section of the supermarket!" he snapped.

The rest of the day went downhill from there. Someone who claimed to be writing an unauthorized biography of Molly V called, demanding an interview. The editor of a well-known woman's magazine called asking him to pose in nothing but a stethoscope for a feature to be titled "The Sure Cure for What Ails You."

A fourteen-year-old patient—female—asked for his autograph. A twenty-three-year-old patient—male—asked for Mallory's telephone number.

A near-hysterical Lori showed up late in the afternoon, providing an explanation about where the press had gotten the photograph of him and Mallory. It seemed she'd been unable to resist showing around school the Polaroids she'd taken. A friend had asked to borrow one over the weekend, then sold it.

David did his best to comfort his crying half sister, assuring her that he knew she'd never deliberately do anything to hurt him—or Mallory. He breathed a silent prayer that she apparently had refrained from bragging about her knowledge of Mallory's actual whereabouts.

Afterward, he called Mallory and said he wasn't going to be able to see her that evening. He explained about the photograph and his fruit section remark.

Mallory said she understood . . . all too well.

As soon as she let him in the next night and saw his face, she knew her estimation that he wouldn't like the experience of going through the media meat grinder had been pitifully optimistic. He looked furious. The warmth, the compellingly male gentleness that had initially attracted her, were gone. He was like dry ice: freezing cold and capable of burning.

He thrust a folded newspaper at her. "Something for your scrapbook," he announced.

The anger in his voice made her wince, but she tried not to take it personally.

The front page of the tabloid was as bad as she expected. It was a cut and paste composite photograph of the two of them. The picture of her was several years old. She wondered if the one of David dated from his appearance at the White House. She let the newspaper drop to the floor.

David glared at her. "A picture is worth a thousand words, hmm?" he asked furiously. "Well, in case you're at all interested, the thousand words in that particular publication say I'm either the lover who replaced Colin Swann in your bed or the dedicated doctor who cured you of some rare and supposedly incurable disease."

Brushing by her, he stalked into the living room. He honestly didn't trust himself to be too close to her at this moment.

He could *feel* her following behind him. Angry as he was, he was still conscious of her subtle, seductive scent and he could visualize the graceful way—

Lord, what had she done to him? What had he done to himself? He'd lost control of his personal life almost from the moment he'd seen her in the supermarket. Everything he'd felt in that first instant—the passion, the protectiveness, the possessiveness—had taken root and grown. Those feelings were an inextricable part of him now.

But his work as a doctor and his devotion to the practice of medicine and to his patients were an inextricable part of him, too. And they had come first due to a promise a grief-stricken fourteen-year-old boy had made himself.

"David," Mallory began, struggling with a sense of guilt and hurt. "David, I'm so sorry. I tried to tell you—"

He turned on her. "Yes, you did try to tell me," he agreed. "But I, the good Lord help me, thought you were exaggerating. You said reporters would be crawling all over me if people found out about us, if I recall. Well, they have been. They've also been crawling through my garbage can, around my kid sister, and in and out of my waiting room. Having my personal life dissected for public consumption is one thing, but this is affecting what I do professionally!"

"I understand—"

"Do you? Do you understand that I had a ten-year-old boy get so overexcited by what was going on yesterday morning, that he had an asthma attack in the examination room? Do you understand that I wasted thirty

minutes doing a case history on somebody I thought
needed medical help only to discover it was *my* case
history the man was after?"

"David—" she put a hand on his arm.

He shook it off. It was time to be totally honest. "I
told you I decided to become a doctor when I was fourteen. The year my mother died. What I didn't tell you
was that she died because her doctor—someone she
trusted and depended on—diagnosed her incorrectly. And
then he prescribed the wrong treatment. If he'd caught
it in time ... But her doctor had personal problems, you
see. He had his mind on something other than medicine.
I know this because my father brought a malpractice suit
against the doctor after my mother died, and everything
came out ... all of it."

There was a pause. Mallory bit her lip. She knew,
with painful clarity, why David was telling her this.

"I knew I wanted to be a doctor before my mother's
death," he went on finally. "After it, I knew what *kind*
I wanted to be."

"The kind who doesn't let his personal life interfere
with his professional one," she whispered.

"Yes." The anger had gone out of him. In its place
was a wrenching, tearing pain. David knew that before
he'd met Mallory he'd been almost completely successful
in becoming the kind of doctor he'd been driven to be.
It had cost him, true, but he'd counted the price as well-
paid, given the return.

At least he'd counted it that way until Mallory had
entered his life.

Mallory was very pale. "You must hate me," she said.

The four words hit him like a body blow. *"Hate you?"*
he repeated. "Mallory, don't you see? I *love* you."

The truth of his feelings burst forth; he flung the words
like an accusation. Whether he was accusing her or himself, Mallory didn't know. Neither did he.

"You ... love ... me?" she asked, taking two steps

away from him. The backs of her legs nudged a chair. She sat down, shaking.

David looked at her, devouring her with his eyes. He ached at the pain he saw in her face. The last thing in the world he wanted to do was hurt this woman and yet he had done just that... and he was going to continue doing it.

"Mallory, I think I've loved you since the very start. I—you've filled up places in me I didn't even realize were empty. That night... the first night we made love ... when I came back from the hospital and found you waiting for me—do you have any idea how right that felt? It was like being given a gift I hadn't known I needed. Or wouldn't let myself admit I did."

He crossed to her and knelt down, taking her hands almost just the way he had the day he discovered she was Molly V. Whether by accident or design, Mallory was wearing the same deep-rose silk blouse she had on the night they had become lovers. Slowly, almost reverently, David undid the right cuff and peeled it back. Bending his head, he kissed the angel tattoo on her inner wrist. His mouth lingered on the mark so long Mallory wondered if he were trying to obliterate it.

"David—" She touched the back of his head gently, her fingertips registering the crisply vital texture of his thick, brown-blond hair. Tears pricked at the corners of her eyes. "David, I love you, too," she said. "And I do know how right it felt that night because for me... for the first time in a long, long time... I felt like I was home."

His head came up. Her words touched off an explosion of joy inside him. Yet, at the same time, they made the wrenching, tearing pain even worse. Dr. David Lenox Hitchcock felt as though he were being ripped in half.

"Oh, Mallory... Mallory... if it was just the two of us, I'd say damn the publicity and the press and everything else. I'd say marry me or live with me... *be* with me for the rest of our lives."

"You—marry you?" Mallory knew she was being given a gift she needed and wanted. She also knew that gift was going to be snatched away. Unless...

He nodded. "Yes. But it's not just the two of us, and we both know it. You once said we were from two different worlds—"

"The doctor and the rock star."

"The doctor and the rock star," he agreed, sandwiching her hands between his palms. "Mallory, I love you. I love *you*. But this—the rest..."

"You mean, Molly V."

It wasn't what he meant—exactly. But it was close enough.

"Yes."

Mallory took a deep breath. "Supposing Molly V quit?" she asked. "Do you think the doctor and the ex-rock star could get together if they lived in the same world?"

- 8 -

"QUIT." BERNIE'S VOICE was so soft Mallory had to strain to hear what he was saying. His breathing was almost more audible than his words. Mallory knew that was the worst possible sign. "You want to quit."

"Yes." Mallory glanced over at David. They were still in the living room of the condominium. She was curled up in the corner of the sofa with the phone cradled between her chin and shoulder; he was sitting a few feet away. They'd talked long and hard before she'd made this call, but they'd both agreed it seemed to be the only way.

David saw the strain on her face. He mouthed the words Are you okay? She gave him a fleeting smile.

"Why, Molly?"

"Mallory."

"What?"

"My name is *Mallory,* Bernie, not Molly."

There was a brief pause. "All right, Mallory. Tell me *why.*"

"I've already told you. At least four times."

"You think you're in love with this Dr. David Hitchcock and you're going to marry him."

"I don't *think;* I know. I've known in my heart for a long time. This is what I—we—want."

"You told me once you wanted to be a star. The first time we met, remember? You told me you'd do anything to make it with your music."

"I made a mistake."

"You've invested ten years in that 'mistake.'"

"Well, I don't want to invest anymore. Don't you understand?"

"It's because of the publicity, isn't it?" Bernie asked, switching direction suddenly. "I saw that wire photo of the two of you. He's a good-looking guy. Solid. Dependable. A real pillar of the community, I'll bet. Nothing like Bobby."

Mallory's stomach clenched. "No, he's nothing like Bobby," she agreed steadily. "Bernie—"

"And I don't suppose the idea of being Molly V's latest exactly appealed to him."

"You have a rotten way of putting things!" she flared.

David got up and moved next to her, slipping an arm around her shoulder. He didn't know what this Bernie McGillis was saying to her, but it was obvious she was hurting. The urge to protect surged in him. "Mallory, do you want me to—"

She shook her head, giving him a look like the one she had given him when he'd come to her aid at the record store. "I've got to take care of this myself," she whispered, covering the mouthpiece with her hand. She was grateful for his willingness to help, but she did have to do this on her own. It was nothing she could explain; she just knew it was important that she did.

"Mol—Mallory?" Bernie's voice went up a few decibels.

"I'm still here. And still that was a rotten thing to say."

"Reality can be rotten, babe. So just what is it you want from me? My blessing?"

"I thought you could help handle the announcement. You *are* still my manager."

"You think all you've got to do is make an announcement that Molly V is packing it in to get married and bingo!—everything's going to be happily ever after time? Honey, you are way beyond *Good Housekeeping* fantasies. You're into fairy tale territory."

Mallory swallowed hard and looked at David again. "I—we—know there will be publicity at first—" She and David had talked about that, too.

"*Publicity?* It'd be worse than after Bobby got himself killed!"

"But it wouldn't last. You yourself told me that people would lose interest in me if I stayed out of the spotlight, remember?"

Bernie swore. Several times. "Okay," he said finally. "Okay."

"Then you'll make the announcement?"

"I'll—a press release isn't going to cover this, babe."

"Why not?"

"Mallory, you know as well as I do the rumors that have been floating around since Bobby died. If you suddenly up and retire, I can guarantee you you'll have reporters digging around until doomsday to get the real story. That Hitchcock's a doctor doesn't help."

Mallory remembered what David had said about the tabloid story. There was more than a kernel of unpleasant truth to what Bernie was suggesting.

"What do you think I should do, then? Call a news conference?" Her distaste for the idea was clear from her tone. She saw David's brows come together.

"Well . . . what about doing a good-bye gig? Going out in style? Let everybody see Molly V's quitting at the top because she wants to, not because she's freaked out, or broken down, or cracked up."

"A good-bye gig?"

"We wouldn't bill it like that," Bernie went on. "But, after the fuss was all over, we could break the story. Hell, it'd be a real classy exit. You could be a rock version of Greta Garbo."

"Bernie, I'm not quitting to become a recluse."

"Yeah, yeah. You're quitting to become a normal person."

"I am a normal person! I just want to be able to live like one."

"All right. Fine! What about the gig?"

Mallory turned the notion over in her brain. It had a definite appeal. It *would* be a classy exit, she thought. And Molly V—*she*—deserved that. She might not like some of the things her career as a rock queen had done to her, but she was proud of her musical accomplishments.

She looked at David. She wanted him to be proud of those accomplishments, too.

"How long would this take to put together, Bernie?" she asked.

"As a matter of fact . . . Nightshade is coming to Hartford this weekend. Do it with them."

Nightshade! She'd completely forgotten about that. To perform with Coney, Boomer, Rick . . . and Colin . . . again—yes, that would be something special.

"Would they mind?" she asked.

"Mind? Hell, no. They'd welcome you back with open arms. I'm not saying this first tour of theirs isn't going well, but you know how first tours are. A little bit of the old Molly V magic wouldn't hurt. It'd be good for you and good for them. I mean, I know how you feel about the guys—"

Yes, Bernie knew, Mallory thought. And he'd traded on that knowledge more than once in the course of her career. He was probably trading on it now, but she didn't mind. Doing the good-bye gig with Nightshade was going to get her what she wanted, and that was what counted.

"Set it up, Bernie," she said.

"Mallory, are you absolutely sure about this?" David asked many hours later, as they lay together in bed. He levered himself onto one elbow and gazed down at her, his face full of tender concern. At the same time, he experienced an almost primitive satisfaction as he took in the lingering signs of the effect his lovemaking had had on her: Her cheeks were still flushed, her lips were faintly kiss-swollen, and her expression was one of sublime satisfaction.

"I'm sure," she told him, reaching up to trace the crease along the left side of his mouth. "Aren't you?"

"Oh, yes." Turning his head slightly, he nipped at the tip of her finger. "I'm sure."

She shivered voluptuously as she felt his free hand stroke her torso and claim one of her breasts. The sensitized tip sprang erect instantly, pressing boldly against his palm. The nipple of her other breast pouted yearningly for equal attention.

"The rock world's loss is definitely your gain," she told him, skiing her nails lightly down his neck and chest.

For some reason he couldn't understand, much less put into words, the remark bothered David—especially since he realized she was quoting him.

"I appreciate what I've got," he replied quietly, and covered her soft, rosy lips with his.

But somewhere in the back of his mind, he wondered if he really did.

"I am going to die," Lori Hitchcock declared in a burst of adolescent overstatement as she trailed Mallory

and David into the Hartford Civic Center four days later.
"I am really going to die."

David and Mallory exchanged looks. Lori had been
issuing variations on this announcement for the better
part of an hour.

"If you die now," Mallory said reasonably, biting the
inside of her cheek to keep from smiling, "you won't
get to meet Swann."

"Colin Swann. Ohmigod." For a moment, Lori seemed
on the verge of hyperventilation. Her blue eyes were the
size of pie plates and her short curly hair seemed to be
standing on end. "Do I look okay?"

"You look fine, Lori," David assured her. His half
sister was wearing the neon green dress and electric blue
earrings he had given her for her birthday.

"I don't want to look *fine*," Lori protested. "I want
to look *hot*. I mean, this is just the most exciting thing
that's ever going to happen to me and if I look like some
kind of nerd or geek—" She made a moaning little sound
of distress. "Oh, maybe I should have worn jeans like
you, Mallory."

Privately, David didn't think anybody could wear jeans
like Mallory. The pair she had on at the moment had
been faded and softened by repeated washings and clung
to her body like melted butter. She was wearing a pale
blue shirt she had borrowed from his closet and her exotic, high-heeled boots. Her yellow down jacket was
slung over her shoulders.

"Lori, you look terrific," Mallory said. "Trust me. In
fact—"

"Molly! Babe!"

This enthusiastic but faintly harried salutation came
from a slightly overweight, balding man in his fifties
who looked as though he'd crawled into his clothes after
spending the night sleeping on top of them.

"Bernie!" Mallory flashed a brilliant smile. "My manager," she clarified for David.

Bernie hustled over. "You made it," he observed un-necessarily.

"I said I'd be here," Mallory replied calmly. "What did you think I was going to do? Pull a no-show?"

"No, no. You're a pro, babe. You always have been. But you know me, I worry a lot." He rolled his eyes, then focused on David. His expression was distinctly assessing.

"David, I'd like you to meet Bernie McGillis, my manager," Mallory said. "Bernie, this is Dr. David Hitchcock and his sister, Lori."

The two men shook hands.

"Mr. McGillis," David said pleasantly.

"Bernie. Glad to meet you, Doc," the manager returned. "I've heard a lot about you." He nodded briefly at Lori who smiled back. "Good to meet you, too, kid."

"Is everything okay, Bernie?" Mallory asked.

"Yeah, yeah. Just the usual headaches. You know how it is. Look, the guys are all inside waiting—"

"Lead the way."

They walked into chaos. Controlled, constructive chaos, to be sure, but chaos nonetheless.

"My God," David muttered under his breath as an ear-splitting shriek of feedback screamed out of a massive bank of speakers to his left. He'd seen hospital emergency rooms that were oases of calm compared with this.

The arena where the Nightshade concert was to be held was huge, and it was crawling with people. People yelling. People screaming. People hammering, hanging lights, and moving things around. People running back and forth at the direction of other people. It was like an electrified ant hill.

David looked curiously at Mallory. She had her head bent slightly to one side to hear something Bernie McGillis was telling her. Except for a faint flush of excitement on her cheeks and a certain sparkle in her wide eyes, she seemed unfazed by the madness going on around her.

"Hey-hey-hey! Moll—ee!"

At this, Mallory whirled, her lips parting in a glowing smile. "Boomer!" she exclaimed happily just a moment before she willingly surrendered to a tidal wave embrace from a red-haired man whose family tree had to include a grizzly bear on one of its branches.

"Hey, Moll, what the hell happened?" Albert "Boomer" Jankowski, Nightshade's drummer, demanded as he deposited Mallory gently back on her feet. "You look terrific!"

"Great line, Boomer," a tall, lanky man with shoulder-length blond hair drawled, joining the reunion. "Did you think it up all by yourself?"

"Rick!" Mallory threw her arms around the band's bass guitar player. She hugged him affectionately, then looked beyond him to a third man. "Coney!"

Coney Guarino, the band's keyboard man, ambled up in the other two men's wake and kissed Mallory warmly on both cheeks. The oldest and shortest member of the group, he had the dreamy-eyed face of a poet punctuated by an incongruous graying Zapata mustache. "Don't mind Boomer, Molly," he counseled in a gravelly voice. "Believe it or not, he's been working real hard on his manners this tour. We've got him trained so he's taking his meals in a bowl now, not scarfing the food up off the floor."

Mallory shook her head at the familiar give-and-take. Coney and Rick had been verbally ganging up on Boomer ever since she'd met them. She went up on tiptoe to give the drummer a quick kiss on the chin. That was as high as she could reach without a stepladder. "That's okay, Boomer," she said reassuringly. "I know what you meant."

"Hey, I said what I meant," the drummer stated, crossing his bulging-muscled arms across his equally bulging-muscled chest. He was wearing a ragged, short-sleeved sweatshirt. There was a garish tattoo of an angel on his left forearm. "You look fantastic. And if these clowns want to make something out of it, let 'em."

Mallory laughed. "Honestly, you three never change."

It was just like old times, she thought humorously, then grew serious. Well, not quite like them. Bobby was no longer there to share in the raillery. A fleeting sadness shadowed her gamine features.

"Hey, when you've got an act that works, you stick with it," Rick said, preening theatrically. He raked his fingers through his shaggy hair. "But Boomer's right— for once. You do look great."

Mallory's face cleared. "Thanks. I feel that way, too." She gave the three men a brilliant smile then turned to David and Lori. "I want you to meet Dr. David Hitchcock and his sister, Lori. David, Lori—this is Boomer Jankowski . . . Rick Nichols . . . and Coney Guarino. Formerly of Fallen Angel, now of Nightshade.

There was a general exchange of greetings. Something in the other men's eyes made David think of the panel that had administered the oral examination for his medical license. He remembered what Mallory had said about considering the band her family.

"Is this a private reunion or can anyone join?" a husky, male voice asked suddenly, interrupting the general air of conviviality.

Mallory turned around. "Swann!"

"Hello, Mallory,"

They embraced. While they did, David took a good look at Colin Swann, the memory of the tabloid story he had read less than a week before stabbing at him with unexpected sharpness.

Colin Swann was in his mid-thirties. He was panther-lean with pitch-black hair and light gray, almost silvery, eyes set under dark, distinctive brows. He kissed Mallory on the cheek before letting her go.

"It's good to see you again, babe," he told her.

Mallory nodded. "It's good to see you, too," she said sincerely. "I want you to meet my . . . friend . . . Dr. David Hitchcock." For a moment, she wished she hadn't gone along with Bernie's suggestion that she keep her plans with David under wraps until they'd worked out all the details of her retirement announcement. "David, this is Colin Swann."

"Mr. Swann," David said.

"Dr. Hitchcock," Swann acknowledged with a cutting smile.

"And this is David's sister Lori," Mallory went on with a slight but significant lift of her brows.

Swann picked up the hint and turned his smile and his silver eyes on the plainly awestruck teenager. Lori melted under the impact of his charm like a popsicle in a heat wave. "Nice to meet you, Lori."

"It is?" Lori asked. She swallowed several times, opened her mouth to speak again, then shut it. Mallory and David exchanged faintly amused looks. It was a rare situation that could render Lori speechless. Coney, Boomer, and Rick seemed to take Lori's reaction as perfectly normal.

"Look, I hate to break up all this chitchat," Bernie cut in sharply. "But don't you think you should try to get in a little rehearsal time? This is going to be an important gig tonight."

"Yeah, yeah, yeah, Bernie," Rick drawled. "Don't sweat it, man. We'll do just fine."

"We're not exactly breaking in a new act here," Coney added, stroking his mustache with his finger.

"We should at least run through the set once," Swann said.

Mallory looked at David apologetically. "This shouldn't take too long—" she began, torn between a desire to share everything with him and her ingrained professionalism. She wondered what he was making of all this . . . and of her part in it. She hadn't missed his reaction when he'd first come into the arena.

"I'll be here when you get back," he told her.

Smiling, she instinctively turned her face up to him.

He kissed her, hard and swift, on the mouth.

"So it's like that, is it?" Swann said in an undertone as he took Mallory's arm and led her off toward the stage. Boomer, Coney, and Rick followed after them.

Mallory smiled, the branding press of David's lips still lingering on hers. "Uh-huh."

David watched curiously for the next few minutes as Mallory was passed around the arena like a tray of hors d'oeuvres, listening with only half an ear to the nonstop commentary being given by Bernie McGillis. He didn't need the manager to tell him how popular Mallory was with the tour road crew and technical staff. Everyone seemed to want to talk to her.

"Look, Doc, I've got some calls to make, if you don't object," Bernie said finally, looking at his wristwatch. He reached into the inner pocket of his wrinkled sports-coat and pulled out two laminated, purple rectangles with thin white elastic cord threaded through them. "These are special guest passes," he explained, handing one to David and the other to Lori. The teenager clutched hers with an ecstatic sigh. "Put them on and nobody will hassle you. Your seat numbers are on them, if you want to watch the concert from out front. They'll get you back-stage with no problems, too."

"Thank you," David said.

"Yeah, thanks!" Lori emphasized.

"My pleasure," Bernie said, waving their appreciation aside. "Why don't you find a place to sit down and relax? They'll start rehearsing soon. If you're hungry—"

"We'll be fine, Mr. McGillis," David told him quietly.

"I can't believe this," Lori said as the manager walked swiftly away. "Is this amazing or what, David?"

"It's amazing," he agreed, still watching Mallory.

Six hours later, Mallory looked in the mirror of her dressing room and Molly V looked back.

She'd thrown everybody—the makeup artist, the hair

stylist, the dresser, the go-fers, even Bernie—out of the cluttered cubicle more than an hour before. She wanted to do this alone, by herself—her way.

The butterflies in her stomach turned to B-52s as she continued studying her reflection.

Ready or not, she thought, here I am.

Closing her eyes, Mallory took one deep, cleansing breath. Lori was somewhere backstage she knew, remanded into the custody of a roadie who was certifiably nonlecherous when it came to girls. David was sitting out front. Mallory didn't know whether he'd elected to see the concert from there to spare his nerves or hers.

At least she could look forward to being with him when she got off stage.

She opened her eyes and glanced in the mirror one last time.

Oh, yes, here I am, she thought with a crazily familiar sense of excitement and trepidation. And I am definitely ready.

Her dark hair had been brushed to a sensuous wildness—untamed, but definitely touchable. Smoky shadows, smudged liner and five coats of black mascara lent a come-hither emphasis to her eyes. A ripe, rose-wine lipstick turned her mouth into an invitation.

Her outfit was similar to the one she'd worn in the days before she'd made it big: a black, tight-fitting jacket with the Fallen Angel motif embroidered on it, and a short black skirt. The difference was that in the old days, the skirt and jacket had been made of black denim and the embroidery had been done by a place that specialized in personalizing bowling shirts. Now her outfit was made of sensuously supple Italian leather and the embroidery was handsewn in brilliants and bugle beads.

After five minutes under the lights, the jacket would come off to reveal a backless halter top, also embroidered with brilliants and bugle beads.

She slipped her sheer-stockinged feet into a pair of outrageously high-heeled shoes. She smoothed a non-existent pucker from the nylon on her left calf and gave a final twitch to the hang of her skirt.

"Molly!" Her manager's voice came through the door. "Show time."

She walked to the door of the dressing room and opened it.

"It's Mallory, Bernie," she said.

"Whatever," he responded, clearly occupied by other things.

Mallory realized with a start that her manager was nervous. She knew he was nervous because his balding forehead was sweating and because his exceptionally ugly purple knit tie—which would normally be merely rumpled like the rest of his wardrobe—was now twisted into something resembling a mutant pretzel.

Bernie took her arm and began maneuvering her toward the wings. "Okay, you know what Swann's going to say when he introduces you, right?" he asked.

"Yes." She flashed a wickedly dazzling smile at a male reporter who had once followed her into a women's restroom in pursuit of a story.

"And you're clear on the order of the songs?"

"Yes." Out of the corner of her eye, she saw Lori Hitchcock. The teenager was staring at her. So was nearly everyone else backstage.

"I put 'Tumble to Earth' near the end to give you a chance to get warmed up. That two octave jump—"

"I understand, Bernie." She made an experimental run down and up the front of her jacket with the zipper tab.

"I've got one of the security guys keeping an eye on your doctor," Bernie went on. "You just think about getting on, getting off, and getting it right."

She looked at him. "I know what I have to do."

Ninety seconds later, she went out and did it.

* * *

What she did was a revelation to David. It was the transformation in the record store magnified to the tenth power and backed by a talent that took his breath away. He'd heard her sing on her albums—even once or twice at the condo during the past few days—but this . . . *this* was something entirely different.

She was entirely different.

Or maybe she had always been this way, but he'd been too caught up in his feelings to see it. Oh, he'd caught flashes of it—his impression of her as an exotic and contradictory creature—but he'd never dreamed . . . he'd never *understood* . . .

She threw back her dark tumble of hair as she threw out the chorus of a song that echoed with the pain of a twelve-year-old orphan whom no one wanted:

> "Baby, don't you remember what's her name?
> What's her name was me.
> Yes, the woman you want is the very same
> Girl you never used to see."

David ached—physically ached—as her crystalline clear soprano melted into smoky sultriness as she began a duet with Colin Swann. Like Mallory, he was dressed in black—black, skin-tight jeans and a black leather vest. A silver stud winked in the lobe of his right ear. He handled his guitar with a caressing confidence, coaxing the music out of it. His voice had a gritty huskiness. Mallory sang:

> "So when twilight starts to fall,
> That's the time I'll come to call.
> The price I ask of you is small—
> But pay it you will."

And Colin sang back:

"Oh, they say she uses witchcraft.
Her touch is magic, she makes grown men cry.
She's a bona fide enchantress.
She's got the devil in her big brown eyes."

She looked so right up there. So vibrantly beautiful. Whether she possessed the music or it possessed her, David wasn't certain, but her control was absolute. She brought the audience to its feet, screaming, with one song, then soothed them to a hushed silence with the next.

The rock world's loss is my gain, he thought.

God, how easily, how arrogantly he'd said those words! To hell with the rock world's loss—what about hers? He'd talked about *his* work, *his* career, *his* professional life—what about hers? He'd been ready to let her sacrifice . . . everything.

And he'd thought of her dead husband as a selfish bastard. At least Bobby Donovan had helped Mallory achieve her dreams.

The doctor and the rock star. They *were* from two different worlds.

Backstage afterward, it was madness.

Mallory was exhausted yet exhilarated. She felt weary one second and ready to light up like a live wire the next. There were purple spots dancing in front of her eyes and her ears were ringing. Her throat hurt and her skin felt as if it didn't fit right. But Lord, how she'd sung!

She wanted to go to David. To hold and be held. But he was standing, off to the side, watching as he had in the record store, and she was hemmed in by a pressing, sweating, shouting bunch of people who all wanted a piece of her. She smiled at him. He smiled back, briefly, and nodded.

"How did it feel to be back in the spotlight, Molly?" someone shouted.

"Amazing," she answered honestly, tearing her eyes away from David's. It would have to be enough, for now, to know he was there. "There's nothing quite like singing in front of a live audience." She laughed. The silver beads on her top flashed icy shards of fire as her breasts rose and fell. "And the audience tonight was definitely live."

"What was going through your head out there?" somebody else asked.

"I was hoping I wouldn't fall off my high heels and break my neck," she replied with another laugh.

"Seriously—"

"Seriously, I wasn't thinking. I was *feeling*. I was flying. Being with Coney, Boomer and Rick again was a high. When things work the way they did tonight—" she trailed off, the residual electricity from the performance still dancing through her nervous system. What had Bernie said she was like on stage? A lightning rod?

"What about being with Colin Swann?" This question, edged with innuendo, came from the back of the crowd.

Mallory tossed her head. "A girl could do a lot worse," she answered.

"Is Molly V joining Nightshade?"

"I—" She glanced toward David again, shivering a little. She must have perspired off five pounds and her sweat-slick body was beginning to cool down rapidly despite the heat generated by the crush of people around her. "I—you'd have to ask Nightshade about that." Bernie had told her it would be best to finesse questions about her future this evening, and finesse them she would. But, Lord, how she wanted to tell everyone the truth and be done with it!

"Doc?"

David was so caught up in his own turbulent thoughts—
and in trying to hear what Mallory was saying—that he
didn't immediately realize that Bernie McGillis had appeared by his elbow. When he finally did, he turned, his
blue-gray eyes distinctly questioning behind his glasses.

"Yes?" he replied.

Bernie smiled fleetingly. "I'm glad you got backstage
okay." He glanced pointedly toward Mallory. "Look, she's
going to be at that for a while. Why don't we go to her
dressing room? You can wait for her there. It's a lot less
crowded and a lot more private. I mean, nobody's picked
up on your being here yet, but—" He shrugged, his voice
trailing off significantly.

"Mallory—?"

"She'll be okay, Doc. She's a pro."

The door to Mallory's dressing room was labeled
MOLLY V and bore a gold star. Bernie nodded casually
at the uniformed security guard sitting next to it as he
let himself and David inside.

"So—can I offer you something to drink?" he asked
pleasantly, waving his hand at the well-stocked portable
bar tucked into one of the corners of the room.

David shook his head, shoving his glasses up into
place on the bridge of his nose with a reflexive poke of
his index finger. "No, thank you."

"Well, if you don't mind, I'm going to have something—for medicinal purposes only, of course." The
manager proceeded to fix himself a Scotch and water.
"Cheers," he said, raising the glass to David before taking
a sip.

David nodded, sitting down on the tweed sofa opposite
the door. He looked around the room curiously. He noted
Mallory's down jacket draped carelessly over the back
of a chair and her high-heeled boots sitting on the floor.
The faintest hint of her perfume lingered in the air.

"What did you think of the concert?" Bernie asked,

settling himself on the edge of the cosmetics-strewn dressing table next to the portable bar.

David looked at him for a long moment. He suspected he knew what Bernie was about to say. He also suspected that it wasn't much different from what he had been saying to himself for the past two-and-a-half hours.

Everything he'd felt during Mallory's performance had been reinforced by what he'd heard her telling the reporters afterward. She *had* been flying tonight. She'd shone out there in the spotlight as she soared with her music. What did he want to do? Clip her wings permanently?

It wasn't a very pleasant thing to discover that a part of him wanted to do just that.

"I thought Mallory was remarkable," he said finally. "I've never been much of a fan of rock music—"

"Yeah, I hear you didn't recognize her at first."

"I didn't," David replied. "And . . . I didn't realize what she was going to be like tonight."

"She's something special on-stage."

"She's something special off-stage, too."

"Mmm." Bernie took a swallow of his drink. "Maybe too special," he remarked reflectively.

David stiffened. "What does that mean?"

The manager held up his hand placatingly. "Hey, I'm not trying to be offensive, Doc—David, if I may." He grimaced. "I get told I'm offensive without trying, if you can believe that. But . . . you love her, am I right?"

David's mouth tightened. He was willing to concede that Bernie McGillis had a right to be interested in Mallory's well-being and future from a professional standpoint. Perhaps, after eight years of association, McGillis had a right to be interested on a personal level, too. But he wasn't about to concede that the manager had a right to pry into his private affairs. Especially not now.

"Yes," he said tersely.

"And she obviously loves you. That's what this whole quitting number is all about."

David looked at him squarely. "Mr. McGillis, why don't you make your point?"

"Look, you apparently can't live with Mallory's career. I understand that. The press, the pressure—it could very well eat you alive. The point is: After what you saw tonight, do you think Mallory can live without it?"

Nearly an hour later, Mallory stood in front of her dressing room door. The post-performance exhilaration had faded, leaving only a sense of satisfying exhaustion. She felt drained . . . almost numb.

She'd given all she had to give out there tonight. She'd held nothing back. No matter what people said about her after this, they'd have to admit she'd made a classy exit.

And now all she wanted to do was to go home. With David.

If she didn't keel over flat on her face first.

She gave the security guard a weary smile, then opened the door and walked in.

David looked up as she entered.

It didn't matter that the tough-chic leather jacket she'd worn on stage had been discarded in favor of a beat-up purple Nightshade tour jacket she'd borrowed from a gorilla-size roadie. It didn't matter that she'd gotten a towel from someplace and managed to rub off most of the makeup perspiration hadn't already removed. It didn't matter that her hair had gone from artful disorder to just plain out-of-control and that she was barefoot with her high heels dangling from the middle fingers of her left hand.

David had never seen a woman more beautiful . . . or more vulnerable.

He did the only thing he could in that moment. He stood up and opened his arms to her.

She came to him, shoes thudding on the floor in her wake, the jacket slipping off her shoulders. She leaned against him for a long moment, feeling his strength. She hadn't let herself lean on him that first day in the supermarket. Now, for a few seconds, she allowed herself that luxury.

"Mallory—" His voice was low, rumbling in his chest beneath her cheek.

She raised her mouth to him, lips parted, her arms going up around his neck and her body molding itself to his.

He was selfish then, kissing her with a fierce, devouring, almost angry passion. The fingers of one of his hands wove through the silken tangle of her hair. The fingers of the other left a fiery path as they trailed down the naked skin of her back to cup her buttocks.

She emerged from the embrace more than a little shaken. Something . . . something had changed. As tired as she was, she could sense it in the way he'd touched her . . . in the way he was looking at her now.

"David?" she asked questioningly, searching his face for some clue as to what was going on. It was a face she knew as well as her own. Perhaps better. She'd studied it lovingly with her eyes, her fingers, and her lips, learning each unique male plane and angle, each life-revealing line, each expression.

Something *had* changed.

"I thought you were incredible out there tonight," he told her at last.

The intensity of the compliment made her flush. But something else about it, perhaps the carefully controlled way he spoke, made a knot of ice form in the pit of her stomach.

"You—you did?"

"I had no idea what you were like on-stage," he said. "What you could do with your music."

Her flush deepened. So did her uncertainty. Lord,

what was wrong with her? She should be feeling pleasure at his words! Instead, she was feeling an all too familiar sense of fear...

She shook her head once, trying to draw on energy reserves that had long since been depleted. "I wanted you to be..." For some reason, the word proud stuck in her throat. "I wanted you to understand."

"I understand, Mallory," he replied. "Part of me wishes I didn't. But I do understand...now."

The knot of ice in the pit of her stomach was developing some very sharp, very nasty edges. She licked her lips, twisting a lock of hair around one finger. "Now... now I'm the one who doesn't understand," she said.

"Yes, I think you do." Her words to the reporters had been proof of that.

She stared at him. It isn't supposed to be like this, she thought. It isn't!

"Mallory." He said her name quietly, almost regretfully. His blue-gray eyes were very serious. "Mallory, you belong in the spotlight."

- 9 -

SHE STARED AT HIM, wondering suddenly if this was the face he showed to patients when he was giving them bad news. The ice in her stomach was spreading through her bloodstream. She was so cold . . . so tired. All she wanted to do was to go *home* . . .

Wherever that was.

"I thought I belonged with you," she said, speaking the words as though they might break.

The hurt in her voice tore at David, but he told himself that a measure of hurt was necessary for both of them now to save them from overwhelming anguish later.

"What you were tonight on stage—" he began.

Mallory turned away from him.

What she was on stage tonight. So it had come to that.

What she was on stage. How she looked . . . sounded . . . performed.

Molly V.

She had been afraid of this happening from the very beginning and she'd been right to be afraid. David couldn't get beyond Molly V anymore than anyone else seemed to be able to.

I hope you appreciate what you've got, she told him. She'd been teasing when she'd said it. Yet she'd trusted, deep down, that he did.

Well, now he did appreciate her . . . only, apparently he didn't want what he appreciated.

David put his hands on her shoulders. His palms seemed very warm against her bare skin. "Mallory, I saw what you did to that audience tonight. There were moments when people practically stopped breathing, you were so good."

A shudder ran through her. She was only dimly conscious of the passionate sincerity in his voice. Out of the corner of her eye, she caught a glimpse of herself in the mirror. The wild hair. The pale, provocative face. The skimpy top and skirt on the supple body. She saw it all. She also saw the exhaustion and the emptiness . . . saw what she'd done to herself tonight.

David's grip tightened for a fraction of a second. "Look, you can say what you want about Molly V and your image and all the rest of that, but it was you, Mallory— your talent, your music, your ambition, *you*— that people were responding to out there. I was responding to you, too. And when you can make people respond like that—" He searched for the right words and came up with her own. "I heard what you told the reporters after the concert. About how it felt to be back singing in the spotlight again. You said there was nothing like it."

"There isn't," she admitted. She couldn't deny what she'd felt, and she'd felt wonderful singing. She'd been good tonight. She'd been better than she had been in a long time. She'd wanted to be. But couldn't David see what it had cost her?

She turned back to face him. No. No, of course he couldn't. He might be looking at Mallory Victor, the woman he said he knew and loved, but he was seeing Molly V, the star.

Oh, yes, something had changed.

"You don't want me to quit, do you, David?" she asked steadily. A part of her mind was shouting that she should be screaming, protesting—*reacting*. But she'd been down this road too many times; she knew the territory too well.

Bernie McGillis had been right. Molly V always made a difference.

"Not for me—no. To give all that up—" He gestured toward the door . . . toward the stage and the spotlight and the audience.

She opened her mouth to tell him how little he knew about "all that," then shut it again. David clearly had made up his mind about her. And she had her pride, she wasn't going to beg.

She said the only thing she thought mattered, "David, I love you."

His beautifully made doctor's hands—man's hands, lover's hands—clenched once. "For how long?" he asked, his voice flat and tight.

Mallory's brown eyes went wide. They looked huge in the eyeliner and black mascara she hadn't been able to wipe off. "What do you mean by that?"

"If you quit to marry me, how long would it be before you started to think about tonight? About what you did and the way it made you feel?"

You'd be bored out of your mind within six months. Her mind grasped the words without his saying them. She'd been able to ignore the prediction when it had come from Bernie. But hearing echoes of it from *David*, too—

"You said you loved me," she said, evading his question and its implications.

"I do." There was a pain growing in him that he knew his skill at medicine and healing could do nothing to ease. "Too much to let you give up everything you've worked for."

"David—"

He knew from the expression on her face that she was going to tell him she wanted to give it up. Perhaps she even believed it. But he knew the answer to the question Bernie McGillis had asked him.

"It wouldn't work," he said shaking his head. "We're just too far apart. You said it yourself once—"

"We're from two different worlds," she completed in a colorless voice. The doctor and the rock star. She took a deep breath. "I suppose, then, that it's time for me to get back to mine. I guess . . . I guess Lori finally has the answer to her question."

"Lori?"

"Remember? She wanted to know how long I was going to stay in Farmington."

The gutsiness that had carried her through so much started to assert itself. Mallory Victor had scars, yes. There would be fresh ones now on top of the old. But she had strengths, too. Strengths she was only starting to recognize.

"Mallory—" David stopped. Even as he watched, she was drawing herself up, tossing back her hair. It was less than the transformation in the record store and only a shadowy hint of what he'd seen tonight, but he could see her changing.

"Tonight was supposed to be Molly V's good-bye gig," she said in a tone of decision. "It will have to do as the launch for her comeback."

It was only after David left that Mallory remembered she'd wanted to tell him that she'd finally finished the

song he'd picked out on the piano the morning after
they'd first made love.

It *had* turned out to be something different and special
. . . a love song.

But David hadn't stayed around to hear it.

Two and a half weeks later, David Hitchcock sat in
his office, staring unseeingly at the walnut-paneled,
diploma-hung wall opposite his desk. He had given up
any pretense of reading through the patient files his nurse
had put out for him before she'd gone home for the night.

He'd been in his office, alone, for more than an hour,
and the only thing he'd read was an article in the latest
edition of *Rolling Stone*. The article was a glowing re-
view of the Nightshade national tour and its recently
added special guest star Molly V. There was a black-and-
white picture of Mallory Victor and Colin Swann singing
together in the spotlight next to the article.

The picture showed Mallory smiling. David could
even see the tiny chip in her front tooth. She looked
happy.

The digital clock on the bookshelf next to his desk
hummed softly and clicked off the passage of another
minute. David blinked. It was nearly seven. He should
be going home.

Only what would he be going home to? A stack of
unread medical journals he wasn't going to read. A meal,
which was perfectly prepared for him by his housekeeper,
that he wasn't going to eat. A big, crisp-sheeted bed he
wasn't going to be able to get to sleep in.

And memories of Mallory he wouldn't be able to
forget, no matter how hard he tried. Every time he opened
the front door of his house, he thought of how it had felt
to come back from the hospital and find her waiting for
him.

David shifted in his chair, experiencing a painfully
familiar stirring in his body and a tightening around his

heart. Taking off his glasses, he pressed the heels of his hands against his eyes.

He was a doctor. He was a good doctor. That was what he'd set out to become more than twenty years before and he'd done it. Yet something inside him was now asking—no, demanding to know—if that was enough.

You've filled up places in me I didn't even realize were empty. He'd said that to Mallory at the same time he'd told her he loved her and he'd meant it from the bottom of his heart.

But now she was gone and those places were empty again.

She would have stayed, a small voice inside his head reminded him insinuatingly. She was ready to stay.

Oh, yes, she'd been ready to stay. She'd been ready to give up her career for him. But he'd seen what that career meant to her—what she gave to it and got in return. He'd heard what she'd said about being back in the spotlight!

He'd had to let her go.

But, dammit, it had been hard! And it was getting harder with each passing day.

He looked down again at the picture in *Rolling Stone,* his index finger moving to trace the outline of Mallory's face.

She still looked happy.

Mallory was miserable. Being on the road wasn't as bad as she remembered; it was worse. The glimpse of rock-and-roll reality she'd tried to give Lori Hitchcock during lunch the first time they'd met now seemed positively romanticized.

Maybe it was her emotional rawness following the break with David that made the maddening tedium of touring—seeing the same people, singing the same songs, answering the same questions—seem such a soul-grinding, energy-sapping experience. Maybe having been away from the upside-down, inside-out craziness of the rock world for a time had left her vulnerable to the manic changes of mood, the pressures of performing, the utter lack of privacy. Or maybe it had always been this awful.

Mallory didn't know. After nearly a month back out on the road, she didn't know a lot of things. But she did know she was miserable and that she had to do something about it.

She had to do something.

The backstage dressing room where she was sitting seemed to be the size of a Cracker Jack box only she wasn't very much of a prize at the moment. Her vocal chords felt as though they'd been ripped out and replaced by barbed wire. As so often happened on tour, the band and road crews had been passing around a variety of germs, including a particularly miserable cold bug. In Mallory's case, the virus had gone for the throat.

In a strange way, she welcomed the physical discomfort. At least it was temporary and could be treated . . . unlike the emotional pain with which she was trying to cope.

Maybe I should call a doctor, she thought.

But the doctor she needed was hundreds of miles away. And even if he'd make the emergency call, she didn't want his professional attentions.

And he didn't want the attentions of her profession.

She smiled grimly, dabbing at her perspiration-streaked face with a tissue and noting with clinical interest that she was developing circles under her eyes. Up close, they were a mauve, almost Nightshade-purple color, and they went nicely with the new hollows under her cheekbones. She'd lost at least ten pounds—probably more, to judge by the fit of her clothing—since she'd left Farmington. If she took off many more, Bernie would quit bugging her about the lingerie poster idea and start suggesting a deal with some famine relief organization.

Mallory crumpled up the dirtied tissue and tossed it into the overflowing wastebasket next to the dressing table. She massaged her right temple.

The gig had gone well tonight. Three encores well. Nightshade—with special guest Molly V—had knocked them dead in some town in Ohio.

Or was it some town in Illinois?

She made a mental note to look at the phonebook back in the hotel. At least this was a two-night stand, not a single. At least she'd be sleeping in a real room tonight, not in the back of the bus. At least she'd be able to wake up in the same town where she'd gone to bed.

Maybe she'd send David a postcard.

Dear David. I wish you were here—wherever here is.

Love . . . Mallory

Maybe she should send him an autographed picture of Molly V.

Lord, she missed David! She missed him from the moment she got up until the moment she crawled into bed cross-eyed with weariness yet so wound up she couldn't sleep. She had dreams about him. And fantasies, too. Fantasies so real they left her aching with frustration.

Singing helped. Not the audience, not the spotlight, but the simple act of delivering a song. Making music had gotten her through the hard times before; it got her through them now. Singing couldn't stop her pain—but it did help.

There was a sharp rap at the door. "Mallory?"

It was Swann. Even if she hadn't recognized his voice, she would have known who it was by the use of her real name. Swann never called her Molly. Ninety-nine percent of the people she was back to dealing with never called her anything else.

She and Swann had developed a healthy professional respect and a wary liking for each other during work on the "Tumble to Earth" album. Those feelings had deepened into a friendship over the past weeks, although Mallory was never completely sure of where she stood with him. It was difficult to say what went on behind Swann's enigmatic eyes.

He entered noiselessly.

"Where are we?" Mallory asked him, turning around.

His smile was full of comprehension. "Akron."

"Um, I thought it was Ohio," she reaffirmed.

He crossed to a chair a few feet away from her, turned it around, and straddled it. "Do you feel as lousy as you look?" he inquired conversationally.

Mallory managed a strangled laugh. "Have you been taking charm lessons from Boomer?"

"Do you?" he pressed.

For some reason, she suddenly thought of a magazine cover she'd glimpsed at the hotel newsstand when they'd checked in. It had had a picture of her and Swann. She wondered if David had seen it. She hoped not.

"Maybe what I need is some of that no-strings sex you're so famous for," she said with an edge of bitter bravado. "After all, we're supposed to be—"

"Yeah, I saw the magazine, too, Mallory. Sure, I could make love to you and make you feel a little less lonely for a couple of hours. But you and I both know that isn't what you need."

Mallory closed her eyes, feeling more than a little sick.

"Mallory, what are you doing here?" Swann asked after a few seconds.

She opened her eyes. "I belong here," she said, consciously rejecting the idea even as she said it.

"Says who?" His voice was cutting.

She sighed. "Bernie."

"Bernie's your manager. I don't deny you're more to

him than just a ten percent meal ticket, but he's hardly what I'd call an objective observer."

"Bobby . . ."

"Oh, yeah. And everybody knows what a great judge of character he was. Look, I hate to speak ill of the dead and all that, but from what I've seen, about the only really smart thing Bobby Donovan ever did was to marry you and then he was too stupid to know how lucky he was."

I hope you appreciate what you have, Mallory thought and then said, "David says I belong here, too."

Swann remained silent.

"I . . . I was going to quit, you know," she went on after almost a minute. "In Hartford. That—it was supposed to be my good-bye gig. David and I . . ." She bit her lip. "I was going to quit."

Swann's expression didn't change. "What happened?"

Mallory spread her hands. What happened was exactly what she had been afraid would happen. "Molly V, I guess."

There was another pause.

"Why do you do that?" Swann asked finally.

"Do what?" Mallory began twirling a lock of hair around her right index finger. She could see the tattooed angel on her inner wrist.

"You always talk about Molly V like a separate person."

"I feel that way most of the time."

"Mallory, you are Molly V. Oh, you put on a little trash and flash to entice the ticket buyers, sure, but it's still you."

She opened her mouth on an instinctive protest, then shut it again.

Look, you can say what you want about Molly V and your image and all the rest of that, but it was you, Mallory—your talent, your music, your ambition, you—

that people were responding to out there. I was respond-ing to you, too.

Mallory caught her breath. David had said those words to her. She'd heard them . . . but had she understood?

Her talent. Her music. Her ambition.

Maybe David hadn't been looking at his friend and lover and seeing the star and celebrity. Maybe he had simply been seeing the whole woman—something *she* apparently hadn't been doing.

Her talent. Her music. Her ambition.

Maybe Molly V only made a difference to people because she allowed it. She'd accepted a split in her life, with part of her in the shadows and part of her in the spotlight. She'd divided herself, and been left with noth-ing but other people's expectations to hold her together. She'd spent herself nearly empty trying to live up to those expectations.

Her talent. Her music. Her ambition.

Her life!

"Mallory?" Swann asked.

She smiled slowly, the weariness and despondency that had been enveloping her falling away like an out-grown cocoon. In their place she felt the dawning of a new sense of inner sureness and completion.

"It's time for me to stop letting everybody else tell me where *I* belong," she said.

"Have you heard from her?" Lori asked David several nights later as she painstakingly rearranged the food on her plate with her fork.

The teenager had shown up on David's doorstep about an hour and a half before, announcing that she needed advice on some unspecified personal problem. She'd then chattered on about everything but personal matters and shamelessly wangled an invitation to stay to eat. She hadn't even flinched when he'd informed her that Mrs.

Winslow had prepared macaroni and cheese for dinner. Lori loathed macaroni and cheese.

There was no need for David to ask who "her" was.

And there was no need to ask why Lori was asking. David saw his face every morning in the mirror when he shaved.

He'd had only one very indirect contact with Mallory since they'd said their good-byes at the Civic Center. A week before, the administrative director of the health clinic he'd helped set up had called about a letter from a Mr. Bernard McGillis. It seemed that the royalties from a new song written by one of Mr. McGillis's clients were being donated to the clinic. No names were mentioned. They didn't have to be.

"Just thought you'd like to know, David," the director had said.

"Thank you," he'd replied, not trusting himself to say much more—nor to speculate on why Mallory had done such a thing.

"Looks like we've got ourselves an angel, hmm?"

David smiled. Little did he know! And how would Mallory react to that if she heard it? She'd laugh, probably. He closed his eyes.

"David?" Lori prompted.

He looked at her young, concerned face. "No," he said quietly. "I haven't heard from Mallory."

He realized that he should have been prepared for something like this. Lori had exhibited a very uncharacteristic restraint when she'd learned that Mallory was resuming her career. At first he'd thought it was because she'd expected it; after all, Lori had known about Mallory's status as a rock star from the beginning. Now he decided that his half sister had simply been biding her time, gauging *his* reactions and, quite possibly, worrying about them.

"Have you heard from Mallory?" he asked after a moment.

Lori shook her head, poking at her congealing pasta as though it weren't quite dead. "I hope she's okay," she said glumly.

David felt a prickle of alarm. He stiffened. "Why shouldn't she be? The papers—"

"You can't believe everything you read, David," Lori said with a strange inflection. Her tone made his brows come together. Looking up from her plate, she saw his expression. "Mallory said that to me once," she explained. "The day I met her. I was asking about her and Colin Swann."

"Oh." His mind flashed back on the picture in *Rolling Stone* . . . of the image of Mallory and Colin Swann singing in the spotlight.

"I guess I acted real dumb that day," Lori observed, still fiddling with her food. "But I didn't know."

"Didn't know what?"

"What it's like," she responded with maddening adolescent ambiguity. "Being a rock star, I mean. Like, I figured Mallory rode on jets and in limousines. But she doesn't. She rides on a bus. And she doesn't even have her own bus. All she's got is this little room fixed up in the back where she can sleep. I guess it's pretty nice, except Mallory said that after a couple of weeks on the road, she feels like the walls are closing in on her. And sometimes she has to be on tour for *months*."

David set down his fork. Lori's pronunciation of the last word triggered a very unpleasant reaction in him. "What else did Mallory say?" he asked slowly.

"Well, she's been all over the country about a dozen times and she's hardly seen any of it. And she has this house in L.A., but she's hardly seen it, either. I think she feels bad about that. She said it's mostly a tax deduction, not a home."

David nodded.

"And people are always after her, you know? Like when the reporters were after you for a couple of days, only much worse. I mean, I always thought it must be exciting to get all that attention. But Mallory said it's almost scary. Everybody wants a part of her. Only sometimes she's not even sure it's really her they want."

David thought of what he'd seen in the Civic Center and in the record store. Everybody *had* wanted a part of her.

"I guess the music is still good for her. But all the other stuff... I think she was thinking about quitting it when she came here to Farmington. Like this was a quiet place where she could get her head straight about things." Lori prodded her food one last time. "Then she met you, huh?"

The question was lobbed out very gently and very tentatively, like someone tossing a rock into a mine field.

There was no explosion.

"Then she met me," David agreed quietly.

"Are you sure about this?" Bernie McGillis asked Mallory.

They were standing backstage at Madison Square Garden. Out front, a capacity crowd was roaring its approval of the first set of the last concert of the Nightshade tour.

In two songs, Swann would make an introduction, and then the crowd would be roaring for *her*.

Mallory smiled and nodded. "Yes, I'm very sure," she said. Everyone else in this place might look on tonight as the end of something; she knew it was the beginning.

She had lots of beginnings to look forward to.

"I only want what's best for you," her manager said.

"I know that. I only want what's best for me, too. And this is it."

"Quitting?"

"Yes."

"Are you quitting because of David Hitchcock?" There was a strange note in her manager's voice.

"No. I'm quitting because of *me*. I still love David,

Bernie. I think I always will, no matter what. And if there's some way to work it out, I want to make a life with him."

"And if there's not?"

She'd thought about that. The possibility saddened her and even scared her a little, but she knew she would be able to deal with it. "I won't go back on the road," she said. "I won't go back to living my life ... *my* life ... in pieces."

Bernie nodded slowly, obviously wrestling with some decision. On stage, Nightshade was playing the opening chords of the song that preceded her introduction.

"Mallory—" Bernie put his hand on her arm. "I have to ... I have to tell you something about Hartford. About what happened between you and Dr. Hitchcock."

Mallory looked at him, her dominant emotion a sense of surprised pleasure that he hadn't called her Molly. "What do you have to tell me?"

"I think ... backstage after the concert, while you were with the reporters, I told him you couldn't live without your career." He wiped a hand over his balding brow. "I'm a manager; I try to manage things—what can I tell you? I'm—I'm sorry. I was only trying to do—"

"—what you thought was best for me," she finished. Strangely enough, she didn't feel any anger. "But you were wrong."

"I know. I shouldn't have—"

She shook her head, covering his hand with her own. "No, no, Bernie. What I meant was you were wrong when you said I couldn't live without my career—" She flashed a smile. "Without this career, anyway. And David was wrong to believe it when you told him. No matter how things end up between us, that's something *I'm* going to tell him."

"Mallory—"

But Swann was already starting to introduce her.

"Don't worry about me," she said, leaning forward

to brush a kiss on his cheek. "I'm going to be fine. This time I really know what I have to do."

Mallory went through a lot of memories and a lot of silent good-byes as she stood out in the spotlight during the next forty-five minutes. She sang all the familiar songs, making them as fresh and as whole as she felt.

She sang for Bobby Donovan and Bernie McGillis and for the nameless drunk in New Jersey who had once led a chant that made her feel special. She sang for Coney, Rick, and Boomer, who had once made her feel as if she had a family again.

She sang for Swann, still not completely sure what was going on behind those silvery eyes of his.

She sang for Lori Hitchcock and for the assistant manager at the record store at the West Farms Mall. She sang for the audience she could feel watching and listening in the darkness.

And she sang for herself. Most of all, she sang for herself . . . and for the sheer pleasure of making music.

Then the time for familiar songs and silent good-byes was over. At her nod and smile, the members of Nightshade nodded and not-quite-smiled back. They knew what she planned to do.

Mallory waited patiently for the last chord of "Tumble to Earth" to fade away and for the applause to die down. She waited until there was quiet; then she began to speak.

"Thank you," she said huskily. "As you probably know, this is Nightshade's last show—" She paused while the crowd erupted into boos. "For a while," she clarified, pausing again while the boos became cheers. "Yes, they're going to be back. In fact, considering how successful they're becoming, I think you're going to have a hard time getting rid of them!"

There were more cheers and laughter at this. Mallory gestured theatrically at the band, inviting them all to take

bows. After they did, she signaled for quiet once again.
Then she cleared her throat.

"Anyway . . . I've been along for the last part of this
ride, and it's been quite a trip. But the ride's over. I—
it's been a ten-year ride, really. And some of it has been
pretty terrific, thanks to these guys and to you—" She
paused, blinking hard. "But some of it has been not so
terrific. I won't go into details. I mean, you've probably
read about it in the papers, right? And who wants to hear
me talk about my mistakes?"

"Sing!" someone hollered, only to be shushed to silence by those around him.

"I'm getting to that," she promised. "All I want to
say is that this is the end of the road for me. After tonight,
Molly V retires."

The boos were nearly deafening. They rolled out of
the audience in a tidal wave of protest. Mallory stood,
unmoving but not unmoved, letting the noise wash over
her.

Finally, it grew quiet again.

"Thank you—" she acknowledged. "But, no thanks.
Now, before I go . . . I want to sing one more song for
you. It's new. A lot of things in my life are. When I
started writing it, my first thought was that it wasn't the
usual Molly V song. Funny thing is, that's the same thing
my manager and Nightshade thought, too. But . . . all
things considered, I don't want to leave you with the
usual Molly V song. So, if you want to listen, this one's
from Mallory Victor."

At the keyboard, Coney played his part of the intro-
ductory measures with gentle, classical precision while
Swann counterpointed on his guitar with infinite delicacy.
Boomer brushed a whisper-light beat out of his drum set
as Rick picked up the bass line. Then it was Mallory's
turn.

And this time, she sang for David.

"He saw her as a stranger; he didn't know her
    name.
He saw her as a woman, not a prisoner of fame.
He saw inside, to things she'd had to hide—
Through masks that she'd applied.
He showed her something better.
So many thought they knew her; they just saw
    fantasy.
She accepted their illusions, till they seemed
    reality.
But in his eyes, she found to her surprise—
She needed no disguise,
When they made love together..."

When the song was over, the spotlight on Mallory
went off. When it came back on, she was gone from the
stage.

"Come on, Molly! Give us the *real* reason! There's
got to be a *real reason!*"

It had taken a good twenty minutes for the pande-
monium out front to calm down. The insanity backstage
had already lasted twice that long and was still going
strong.

Mallory brushed back her hair, marveling at her calm
in the face of madness. Bernie, ever the manager, had
insisted that she had to give a press conference after the
concert. He'd pointed out that reporters were going to
be backstage to question her whatever she did, so she
might as well answer them on her terms.

"I've already given you the real reason. After ten years
on the road, I'm tired and I want to get off."

"But stars don't just quit!"

"This one does."

"Doesn't your career mean anything to you anymore?"

"Of course. But my health and my sanity mean more."

"But what are you going to do? What *can* you do?"

"You might be surprised," she said. "Look, I don't know how to explain it more than I already have. I'm retiring Molly V. I'm not resigning from the human race. In fact, in a way, I think I'm rejoining it. I'm not going to become a . . . recluse—" She saw Bernie out of the corner of her eye and smiled. "I'm going to keep writing music . . . songs like the last one you heard tonight. And I might do some recording, too. But beyond that—as radical as it may sound—I want to have a *normal* life."

"You don't think that'll be boring?"

"There are worse things than boring, believe me."

"Name one."

"Having to ask somebody what city you're in. Not being able to go grocery shopping."

"Grocery—hey, wait! That's where that what's-his-name—the doctor—he said he met you in the fruit section of a supermarket. You mean he wasn't kidding?"

Mallory hadn't intended to bring David into any of this. "No," she said carefully. "He wasn't kidding."

"Is he the real reason you're quitting? Is he behind this?"

She shook her head emphatically. "No, *I* am."

"Well, how does he feel about what you've done?"

"I don't know."

Two hours later, she had a chance to find out. Because when she got back to her hotel room, David was waiting for her.

- 10 -

HE WAS SITTING on the edge of the bed when she came in. She had the feeling he had been sitting there for a long time, waiting. She had the feeling the wait hadn't been easy.

He got up slowly. Her door key slipped from nerveless fingers as she got her first look at David Hitchcock in more than a month.

"You look awful," she whispered, even as she was drinking in and rejoicing over every feature in his beloved face. He was thinner and there were painfully unfamiliar lines of stress and sleeplessness around his eyes and mouth. The compassion, the intelligence, the gentleness, she had fallen in love with were still there. But there was new vulnerability as well.

He looked like a man who had been questioning the very foundations of his life.

"You don't," he responded quietly. She had lost some weight, yes, and she looked tired, but there was a serenity about her that he had never seen before. And the contradictions he had sensed in their first meeting were gone, too. "You look beautiful."

"Oh, David." And she opened her arms to him.

He came to her, embracing her, adoring her, trying to communicate wordlessly all the things he had to say to her. His body was warm and strong and male against hers.

For a few blissful moments, Mallory lost herself in the feel of him. She melted against him, touching him, stroking him, trying to communicate wordlessly all the things she had to say to him.

But, eventually, they both needed words.

"Why are you here, David?" Mallory asked, pulling back a little. The how of his being here could wait. She was trembling. Her eyes were very bright and her cheeks were flushed. Underneath her fine Victorian blouse—the same blouse she had worn the first night they'd had dinner together—her breasts were taut and aching for his touch.

He released her, shutting his mind to the desire surging through him. "I'm here because I want to try to put things right between us, Mallory. Because I need to put them right. I've made so many mistakes, so many misjudgments about you . . . about *myself*—"

"What do you mean?"

"When I came here tonight, I didn't know what I was going to see when you walked through the door. I didn't know if it was going to be the smiling singer in the spotlight I'd seen in *Rolling Stone,* or the unhappy celebrity Lori told me about."

"Lori?"

"She told me some things you told her about your . . . life. About your bedroom in the back of the bus. About going everywhere but seeing nothing. About everybody wanting a part of you."

Mallory nodded slowly. "I remember what I told her."

"She was worried that you might not be okay."

"I'm okay. I'm more than okay."

"I can see that."

"Were you hoping that I wouldn't be?"

He shook his head quickly. "No. Absolutely not. The last thing in the world I'd hope is that you were unhappy. But I don't deny . . . I don't deny that when Lori told me what she did, one of my first impulses was to take off and come riding to the rescue. I've always had that urge to protect where you're concerned. That day we met in the supermarket, I kept thinking that I wanted to sweep you up and away somewhere. To cherish you. To shield you from whatever was so obviously hurting you."

A strange mixture of emotions assailed her. "Is that what you're here for? To ride to the rescue?" A month ago—even less—she would have gladly accepted his rescue, his protectiveness. But now . . .

"Looking at you, Mallory," David said evenly, registering her new and unexplained serenity once again, "I don't think you need rescuing anymore. Do you?"

She shook her head, her dark hair drifting softly about her shoulders. "No," she said simply. "I've rescued myself."

"From a situation I put you back into . . . because I didn't understand."

"No—" she began protesting, realizing that he was talking about what happened between them at the Civic Center. He had been in the wrong then, yes, but so had she. And if blame were to be apportioned, she deserved part of it.

"Mallory, please," he interrupted. "I want to try to explain why I acted as I did the night of the concert."

She waited a beat. "All right," she agreed. He could

have his say; then she would have hers. And afterward...

David began to pace, marshaling his words. After a moment, Mallory moved and sat down on the edge of the bed where he had waited patiently for her. Once she was still, he began to speak.

"Mallory, it was very easy for me to say yes when you said you'd give up your career," he began. "It was easy because from my point of view, your career was interfering with mine and I've always put mine first. And it was easy because I had no idea what your career really was."

"Until the concert." She thought she knew what was coming.

"Until the concert," he agreed. "I sat in the Civic Center and I watched and I listened and it was...a revelation. Not just of your talent, but of my selfishness and arrogance."

"W—what?" This was not what she had expected at all. "David, you're not selfish—"

"Mallory, I came very close to letting you sacrifice something that must mean a great deal to you without even realizing what I was doing. If that isn't selfish, what is?"

Then she understood why he had acted as he had in Hartford. And she understood that she had misread his motives as badly as he was still misreading hers.

"But you didn't let me," she told him. "If you'd been truly selfish, you would have let me quit there and then in Hartford." A great many men she knew would have done just that. Her late husband Bobby probably would have.

"Don't think I haven't tried to comfort myself with that thought," he responded. "But it goes deeper. Mallory, in all the time we spent talking about what you were going to give up for me, it never once occurred to me to consider what I should be giving up for you."

"I don't want you to give up anything for me!"

"What about my quest to be the perfect, impersonal professional? The one that's made me a damn good doctor but an incomplete human being?"

Mallory started at the pain in his voice. David *had* been questioning the very foundations of his life. She hurt for him, because she knew what it cost to ask—and answer—such questions. She hurt because David felt the need to bare himself emotionally to her, just as he had often bared himself physically. Yet for all the hurt, she knew that this was an act of love and trust from a man whose deepest instincts were to withhold himself.

"David—" Her first thought was to find some way to comfort him. "David, I understand why you feel the way you do about medicine. A lot of people would have turned away from becoming a doctor. They would have become bitter after what happened. But you—"

"But I let myself get caught up in my grief and the obsession of a fourteen-year-old boy. Don't you see? *One* doctor made *one* tragic mistake. And I've compounded it. I've spent more than half my life avoiding involvement and intimacy because I've been scared to death I would repeat that one doctor's one tragic mistake. And then I found you, Mallory. I told you before you filled up places in me I didn't even know were empty. Well, I know it now. After a month without you, I can give you a map of each and every one of those places." He stopped and looked at her, his feelings naked on his face. "It's not just your loving me that fills the emptiness. It's my loving you, too. My God, I love you, Mallory. And I don't give a damn about the doctor and the rock star—about being from two different worlds. I want a chance for us—a man and a woman—to build our own world together. I know it won't be easy. I know that now and then it won't be just the two of us. But I want to try."

Mallory looked down at her hands for several seconds, not trusting her voice.

"Mallory?" David questioned, his heart pounding as he watched her dark, inclined head. He was thinking again of the serenity he had seen on her face when she had come in. Something—or was it someone?—had put that expression on her face. "Mallory, is it too late for us?"

She lifted her head in a graceful movement. "No," she told him with a beautiful smile. "How could it be when I love you, too? It's not too late for us, David. It's just the beginning. But—"

"But—?" Breathless, he came toward her. The serenity had become a kind of radiance from within. There was a glow to her that owed nothing to a spotlight.

"But it is a little late for Molly V. She retired tonight."

"What?" He knelt down in front of her, much as he had done the day he had first learned about Molly V.

"I quit," she said simply. "I quit in Madison Square Garden in front of thousands of people. That's what I meant when I said I'd rescued myself."

He nodded, his hands coming up, palms down, to rest on her blue-jeaned knees.

"I didn't do it for you," she went on after a moment, her body heating hungrily at his touch. "Not in the way I was going to in Hartford. Not in the way the reporters were asking me about tonight, either. I did it for myself, David. I . . . did it out of hope for us, too, in a way. But mostly, I quit for me because it's my career and my life and I have to be the one who makes the decisions in it. And one of the decisions I've made is that even though there *is* nothing quite like being in the spotlight, it's not worth the price I have to pay to be there. It may be to some people, but it's not to me. If I hadn't known that for certain before, I know it after this last month."

"Was it . . . bad for you?" he questioned, thinking that "bad" was pathetically inadequate as a description of the sleepless nights and aching days he'd endured since they'd parted.

"It was hell," Mallory said honestly. "But I survived it and I'm here . . . whole . . . with you." She looked at him, the expression in her eyes promising him the gift of herself and her love. "This is where I want to be, David. This is where I belong."

"*This* is where you belong," he said, and he surged up to meet her gift with his own.

They were both eager the first time. There was an unashamed urgency in each word, each kiss, each touch. Attuned as always, they found a fierce and frantic rhythm that spiraled them up and out of themselves. They shattered together in a crescendo of pleasure that was as intense as it was inevitable.

The second time was much different. Gentle and generous; lingering and loving.

Mallory's hands glided over David's body in rapt exploration, paying tactile tribute to his maleness. She sculpted the breadth of his shoulders and measured the lean length of his arms and legs. Her fingers danced through the rough silk of his chest hair, then chased ripple after shudder down his torso and across the flat plane of his belly.

He captured her breasts in his own hands, holding them sweetly tormented captives until she ransomed them with throaty sobs of pleasure. The satiny globes pouted greedily against his palms, the rosy nipples teased to yearning points.

Delicately, rapturously, he sampled the secrets between her trembling thighs with his fingers . . . and then his lips. Mallory arched up wildly, the burning imprint of his mouth firing her body as though it were dry tinder. She moaned pleadingly as he sought and found her again. His breath was warm and whisper-soft and she thought she felt him smile as he claimed her for a third time.

When he finally entered her, it was with one deep thrust. He sheathed himself fully in the velvet clasp of her femininity. In that moment, there on the edge of ecstasy, conquest and surrender were the same.

Wide-eyed with wonder, Mallory gazed up at David, watching with tender satisfaction as his features grew taut, then flushed. The play of expressions over his face was as arousing as the strong, sure movements of his body over hers. She wrapped her arms and legs around him, her slender fingers digging into firm flesh.

"David, please!" she finally whimpered, her eyes now closed as her head tossed back and forth. She was drunk on the sensations he was evoking in her, but deprived of the final completion she now desperately craved. "Oh, please—"

He said something hoarse under his breath, his body shifting slightly. She felt him balance himself, taut as a bowstring.

Her long dark lashes fluttered open. Blindly, she brought the palm of one trembling hand to lie against his cheek.

"This," he told her on a shuddery intake of breath, "is where *I* belong."

Man and woman.

Whole.

"You never did tell me how you got into my hotel room," Mallory murmured a long time later. David was on his back in a contented sprawl and she was curled against him, her chin resting on his chest.

"You never did ask," he replied, watching her through loving, half-closed eyes. Satiation had chased the stress from his features. The weariness he had seen on hers had been replaced by a voluptuous languor.

Mallory smiled, tracing an ever-decreasing circle around one of his nipples. "How *did* you get into my hotel room?"

"Bernie."

Her finger stopped moving. *"McGillis?"*

He nodded. "I called him about a week ago, after I talked with Lori."

"When you were considering riding to the rescue?"

"Mallory, wanting to get to see you again was more a matter of rescuing myself than anything else."

"What happened?"

"He wasn't particularly cordial."

"And then?"

"And then, three days ago, he called me at my office. He said that if I were serious about wanting to talk to you, he'd arrange for me to see you at your hotel after your concert with Nightshade."

Mallory worried her lower lip for a moment. "Four days ago, I told Bernie I was quitting. He didn't say anything about that?"

David shook his head.

Mallory thought back over her manager's behavior just before she'd gone on stage this evening. "Maybe he thought he'd said enough in Hartford," she commented quietly.

David's naked chest rose and fell as he took a deep breath and slowly let it out. "He told you about that?"

She nodded. "He said he was sorry."

"Maybe letting me in here was his way of apologizing."

"Maybe . . . then again, maybe he was just doing what he always tries to do."

"What's that?"

"What he thinks is best for me." She gave David a faintly mischievous smile. "This happens to be one time when he had the right idea."

"Mmm . . . speaking of Bernie and right ideas. The clinic I work with in Hartford got a letter from one Mr. Bernard McGillis. It seems a client of his—no names, please—wrote a new song and wants to donate the royalties from it to the clinic."

Mallory dipped her head, momentarily veiling her face with her hair. "You weren't supposed to hear about that."

"Hear about what? The donation or the song?"

"The donation." She tossed back her hair and looked at him. "I wrote the song for you," she said.

"Was it the one I saw on the piano?"

She nodded.

"What did it turn out to be?"

"Something special."

He traced the curve of her petal-smooth cheek. "I think I told you I hoped I could hear it when it was finished."

She met his eyes steadily. "Now?"

"Or I'll wait around."

"No . . ." Suddenly, she decided she wanted to sing it for him, like this, in private. Taking a deep breath, she began.

She was a little off key during one verse, and her voice tended to wobble on certain words, but her audience of one was mesmerized, utterly still. There was a beautiful, very tender silence once she finished.

"Thank you, my love," David said finally.

Afraid she might cry, Mallory buried her face in his shoulder. After a moment, she felt him pick up her right hand and kiss the inner wrist where her tattoo was.

"Mallory," he said.

She lifted her head. The man she loved, the man she belonged with, was smiling at her.

"If anybody ever accuses you of being anything but an angel," he told her, "I want you to refer that person to me. I'll set the record straight."

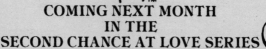

COMING NEXT MONTH
IN THE
SECOND CHANCE AT LOVE SERIES

QUESTIONNAIRE

1. How do you rate _____
                    (please print TITLE)
   ☐ excellent   ☐ good
   ☐ very good   ☐ fair   ☐ poor

2. How likely are you to purchase another book
   in this series?
          ☐ definitely would purchase
          ☐ probably would purchase
          ☐ probably would not purchase
          ☐ definitely would not purchase

3. How likely are you to purchase another book by
   this author?
          ☐ definitely would purchase
          ☐ probably would purchase
          ☐ probably would not purchase
          ☐ definitely would not purchase

4. How does this book compare to books in other
   contemporary romance lines?
          ☐ much better
          ☐ better
          ☐ about the same
          ☐ not as good
          ☐ definitely not as good

5. Why did you buy this book? (Check as many as apply)
          ☐ I have read other
             SECOND CHANCE AT LOVE romances
          ☐ friend's recommendation
          ☐ bookseller's recommendation
          ☐ art on the front cover
          ☐ description of the plot on the back cover
          ☐ book review I read
          ☐ other _____
             _____
             _____

(Continued...)

6. Please list your three favorite contemporary romance lines.

_____
_____

7. Please list your favorite authors of contemporary romance lines.

_____
_____
_____
_____
_____
_____

8. How many SECOND CHANCE AT LOVE romances have you read? _____

9. How many series romances like SECOND CHANCE AT LOVE do you <u>read</u> each month? _____

10. How many series romances like SECOND CHANCE AT LOVE do you <u>buy</u> each month? _____

11. Mind telling your age?
        ☐ under 18
        ☐ 18 to 30
        ☐ 31 to 45
        ☐ over 45

☐ Please check if you'd like to receive our <u>free</u> SECOND CHANCE AT LOVE Newsletter.

We hope you'll share your other ideas about romances with us on an additional sheet and attach it securely to this questionnaire.

• •

Fill in your name and address below:
Name _____
Street Address _____
City _____ State _____ Zip _____

Please return this questionnaire to:
  SECOND CHANCE AT LOVE
  The Berkley Publishing Group
  200 Madison Avenue, New York, New York 10016